unSPARKED

7

FEAR

CORINNA TURNER

unSeen

PRAISE FOR CORINNA TURNER'S BOOKS

LIBERATION: nominated for the *Carnegie Medal Award 2016.*
ELFLING: 1st prize, Teen Fiction, *CPA Book Awards 2019*
I AM MARGARET & *BANE'S EYES:* finalists, *CALA Award 2016/2018.*
LIBERATION & *THE SIEGE OF REGINALD HILL:* 3rd place, *CPA Book Awards 2016/2019.*

Corinna Turner was awarded the **St. Katherine Drexel Award** in **2022.**

PRAISE FOR *ELFLING*

I was instantly drawn in

EOIN COLFER, author of *Artemis Fowl* and former Children's Laureate of Ireland.

PRAISE FOR *FEAR*

Heart-rending and nail-biting, even more than usual!
Good thing I have a strong heart!

KATY HUTH JONES, author of *Treachery and Truth*

Every episode of unSPARKed seems to ratchet the tension up a notch. FEAR takes it up a few. If you thought the characters were in a tough situation before.... Well, just read it and find out.
MARIE C. KEISER, author of *Heaven's Hunter*

PRAISE FOR THE UNSPARKED SERIES

I've long been curious about what sparked Corinna Turner's imagination to somehow think of writing a series that combines faith, action, and dinosaurs. Whatever ignited her creativity, the result is the raptorously fantastic unSPARKed series. The short episodic formula used in these books brilliantly unfolds the story in quick, fast-paced segments.
Beware: this series' vivid descriptions, heart-pounding drama, and fabulous characters are sure to lure you in, as well.

LESLEA WAHL, author of the Blindside series

ALSO BY CORINNA TURNER:

I AM MARGARET series
For older teens and up

Brothers *(A Prequel Novella)**
1: I Am Margaret*
1: Io Sono Margaret (Italian)
2: The Three Most Wanted*
3: Liberation*
4: Bane's Eyes*
5: Margo's Diary*
6: The Siege of Reginald Hill*
7: A Saint in the Family
'The Underappreciated Virtues of Rusty
Old Bicycles' *(Prequel short story)* Also
found in the anthology:
Secrets: Visible & Invisible*

I Am Margaret: The Play *(Adapted by
Fiorella de Maria)*

UNSPARKED series
For tweens and up

Main Series:
1: Please Don't Feed the Dinosaurs
2: A Truly Raptor-ous Welcome
3: PANIC!*
4: Farmgirls Die in Cages*
5: Wild Life
6: A Right Rex Rodeo
7: FEAR
8: A Different Kind of Camouflage†
9: Soil and Leaf†

Prequels:
BREACH!*
A Mom With Blue Feathers†
A Very Jurassic Christmas*
'Liam and the Hunters of Lee'Vi'

FRIENDS IN HIGH PLACES series
For tweens and up

1: The Boy Who Knew (Carlo Acutis)*
2: Old Men Don't Walk to Egypt (Saint
Joseph)*
3: Child, Unwanted (Margaret of
Castello)

Do Carpenter's Dream of Wooden
Sheep? *(Spin-off, comes between 1 & 2)*

1: El Chico Que Lo Sabia (Spanish)
1: Il Ragazzo Che Sapeva (Italian)

YESTERDAY & TOMORROW series
For adults and mature teens only
Someday: A Novella*
Eines Tages (German)
1: Tomorrow's Dead†

OTHER WORKS

For teens and up
Elfling*
'The Most Expensive Alley Cat in London'
(Elfling *prequel short story*)

For tweens and up
Mandy Lamb & The Full Moon*
The Wolf, The Lamb, and The Air Balloon
(Mandy Lamb *novella*)

For adults and new adults
Three Last Things *or* The Hounding of Carl
Jarrold, Soulless Assassin*
A Changing of the Guard

The Raven & The Yew†

† **Coming Soon**
* **Awarded the Catholic Writers Guild** *Seal of Approval*

CONTENTS

DARRYL

"This or a bullet. If you're lucky," says Josh.

Yeah, Jason Desmoines is even now climbing to the top of the second of the two barns that make up his illegal rex battery farm and as soon as he spots us over here on the other barn roof, he'll shoot us—or capture us, which may be worse.

"Weigh the odds," Josh adds. "Trust me, these are better. Let's go."

A lot of juvenile T. rex mill around the open barn doors below us, equal parts frightened and curious about the never-before-seen nighttime world outside. Josh grabs Harry's hand and I grab Harry's other hand, positioning him over a juvenile just below us. That puts me nicely over my target animal.

This is crazy. This is *crazy*.

This is our only chance.

"Three," says Josh. "Two, one, *jump*..."

He jumps. I jump. Harry, thank God...jumps.

My legs land on either side of the rex's neck, its backbone slamming into my sternum and knocking the breath from me. I lean forward and stretch...yes, I can just get my arms around its neck and in the nick of time as it spins around, startled by my arrival. But I weigh nothing compared to its five tons and it's sufficiently used to humans that it doesn't go totally nuts, the way a wild one probably would. Heels, heels...scrabbling around, it seems an eternity but I get them tucked under the rex's stubby arms, as far back as I can. Is that right?

Finally, I manage to spare a glance around me.

Josh appears securely mounted, no surprise. Harry looks, I suspect, rather like me, arms clamped around the creature's neck, heels...yes, hooked in, eyes bulging as the light from the barn catches his pale face for a second. His rex is circling too, also confused by its human passenger.

Josh reaches out and starts giving every rex that's facing the electric fence a real good zap. They roar and start running. I guess they don't even know what the fence is, because they go right through it without any further encouragement. A couple bellow again as they get shocked, but they're already running so they don't stop.

"Come on!" Josh reaches behind him and taps his rex with the prod. With a roar, it charges forward. Harry's follows.

I reach back and tap mine...yes, it's moving. I cling desperately, almost left behind by the acceleration, feeling my legs holding me on, anchored by my heels. Arms wouldn't have been enough.

We're approaching the hole in the fence...but another, larger, juvenile shoulders into mine, snarling. My mount turns aside, swings around, along with some other juveniles, pounding down the side of the barn instead. Not the side closest to the egg barn where Jason is, thank God, but...

Do I try to get it turned around? Or do I just...?

The fence looms dead ahead, freedom just beyond. I reach back and jab the prod into my rex's tail, zapping as long and hard as I can before letting the prod swing on its strap again and grabbing hold to stay on.

Oh heck, the *wires*... I bury my face against the rex's neck and squeeze my eyes closed, the scraggly remains of its juvenile plumage scratching my face. Other juveniles are still running with us. Several roar deafeningly as the fence goes down, something that sparks whisks past close to my ears...and then I'm charging away into the darkness on the back of a T. rex, the camp along with angry Jason and his angry men and his possibly eaten brother falling behind me.

Astonishingly, Josh's plan has worked. More or less. I hope. Did Josh and Harry get out? Their rex were heading straight for the gap in the fence the last I saw. I hope they're okay.

So...as soon as I get out of sight of the camp, I need to get off. Slide down the back, Josh said, then tuck and roll and lie still until the rex are gone. I glance at the boulder-strewn snow flashing past beneath me. It looks an awfully long way down and we're going *really* fast. I'd better wait until they slow up.

Huh, maybe waiting isn't such a good idea. They're just going and going and going. They've never been able to run before and the prods and the fence have filled them with adrenalin. This is no good. I've got to be able to find my way back to the habitat vehicle. If we go much further I'm going to have trouble retracing my steps unless I literally follow the rex prints the whole way and then I'm right there when Jason comes along doing the same thing. I've got to slow my juvenile down—or get off regardless.

I reach out and tug on the rex's crest feathers. It jerks them free at once but breaks its stride to do it, so I grab them and tug again. This time it slows almost to a halt, turning in a circle as it pulls free once more, making fretful noises. Okay, as soon as it's going straight again and not so interested in me...

Freed from the tugging, the rex turns its head after

the others and begins to pick up its pace. I quickly unhook my heels, get the prod in one hand and let myself slide down its back, managing to topple off at the bottom and land curled up on my non-prod-clutching side.

Oof. But the snow broke my fall and I'm off. And the rex...

Steady vibrations against my hip, the only part of me touching the ground through the snowdrift, gradually reduce in intensity. The rex is running on after the others, probably glad to be rid of the strange little creature that was clinging to its neck but more interested in catching up with its mates than in investigating further. Male T. rex, like allosaurs, form bachelor packs for protection until they are adults, when the survivors become strictly solitary, and these juveniles are all young enough to have a strong pack instinct. Luckily for me.

The rex have been following the valley bottom and although they took a couple of forks I think I can find my way back. First, I need to get to the valley side without leaving too many tracks for Jason to find. At the thought of Jason, I grope at my parka, checking the flare pistol remains in my pocket. Yes. And my hunting knife at my belt. Though if I get at close enough quarters with Jason to use *that*...

Hmm. Clouds are starting to cover the moon, but

the lines of rex prints leading back the way we came are still visible, crisp against the otherwise unmarked snow. Odds are Jason and his guys won't be looking closely at those rex prints, they'll just be following them as fast as they can. Since the prints cut very close to the valley side only a few hundred feet from here, I hop from footprint to footprint until I can leap sideways and land in some scrubby undergrowth where my own prints won't be very noticeable.

Phew. Unless they're actively looking for me, they're unlikely to find my trail now. And I'm guessing even if they *did* spot us leaving, they *won't* be actively looking for us just yet. If the Dinosaur Activity and Population department (or DAPdep, as most people call them) notice an extra fifty juvenile T. rex in this region, you can bet Jason's fake hunting camp won't withstand their scrutiny. If he can't catch almost all of those rex, his whole operation is blown. Revenge will take second place to survival—at least for a while. Luckily for us.

I move along the bottom of the slope, trying to get my bearings. The mountain to my left is the one where the HabVi is parked, right? Is it better to follow the valley bottoms back to where we came down, right near the camp, or just head straight up towards it? It looks as though if I went directly up this slope I'd get to some sort of ridge that leads towards our mountain. Retracing my steps will keep me near where Jason will be; cutting upslope will get me further away.

Upslope it is, then. The sooner I get up into higher, craggier ground the less likely I am to meet larger predators, too. Although, even going one on one with a pair of winter-hungry Deinons or a pack of hungry Velociraptors, armed only with an electric prod, a knife, and a flare gun I barely dare fire because of Jason, might not end well.

For me, anyway.

HARRY

I've never known a mile like this in my life. Leaning on me and on his prod, Josh keeps going, step after step, up that mountain. He has his left hand tucked into the breast pocket of his parka, as a makeshift sling. His breathing gets rougher and rougher. Agonized. A rex bite and broken ribs. How much pain is he in?

He's only asked to rest three times, and he clearly isn't getting irrational from shock because he stops only very briefly before plowing onwards.

"It must be much less than a mile now," I tell him. "Much less!"

"Think five," he gasps.

"Five what?"

He's silent as he struggles up a steep part, then finally replies, "Five miles. Equivalent."

He's saying it's the equivalent of walking *five* miles? How did he work that out? I guess one mile for actual distance and one for the altitude grain. Maybe another for the darkness and yet another for the rough terrain. And the fifth? Oh, for Josh being barely able to walk for pain and blood loss. I'm already half-carrying him. Okay, so it's gonna be like going five miles in time and effort. No way have we gone anything close to that, yet. *Outage.*

We're crossing a slightly open area between two crags—I think. The moon has gone behind the clouds completely and the faint red beam from the flashlight clipped to my shoulder doesn't illuminate very far ahead. But I think there'll be no scrambling for a few minutes. Good. Josh is struggling enough as it is.

His parka squishes under my clutching hand as I try to support him—blood smell fills my nose. Yeah, even I can smell it. A raptor will be able to catch the scent a mile away. Or more. The clotting crystals had stopped the bleeding; I hope none of the puncture wounds have opened up again. Would stopping to check do more harm than good? I'd have to get his coat off and expose him to the freezing air again. And every second we're out here smelling like this reduces our chances of making it back to the 'Vi.

"Can you tell if you're bleeding, Josh?"

"Don't...think...so."

"Good."

Scuffing sounds, small rocks bouncing... Something's moving on the other side of the clear area. My hand flies to my shoulder, turning up the flashlight. Knee-high dark shapes move in the light, three pairs of eyes reflect at us and one—

"Eugh!" I recoil, smacking into the rock behind us and dragging Josh off-balance—he grunts and almost falls, catching himself against the crag.

Eyes! The fourth creature has two normal eyes and a body *covered* in smaller eyes, all bouncing the light eerily.

The dark shadows flit onwards...and are lost in the night.

"What the heck was that? Like a...a *short-circuiting* cherubim!"

"Huh?" Josh sounds confused, gesturing for me to turn the light down again—which I do quickly to reduce our loss of night vision.

"Real angels—y'know, as described in the Bible," I tell him, "are, like, covered in eyes. Scary-looking."

"Oh." He sounds exhausted—but totally un-alarmed. Leaning against the rock-face, he breathes heavily for a while before finally saying, "Well, that weren't no angel. Just a momma velociraptor carrying her babies on her back. And three pack members with her."

I tense in alarm, but he gives his head a slight shake. "They weren't hunting. Not with their hatchlings along. Bugging out to get away from some threat. Looking for a new den site. Not interested in us. Only four, anyway. A couple of zaps, a flick of the frights and they'd run."

I finally start to relax too. He's right. We've got the electric stock prods and I'm wearing Josh's frights— mechanical fan-like devices on my arms designed to burst out and startle a predator.

"Ugh, that was eerie," I can't help saying. The darkness makes it worse. Then I wish I hadn't said it in case I sound chicken, so I change the subject quickly. "Early for hatchlings, isn't it?"

"It's just about into the period when you'd expect the very first early hatchers. The rest of the pack were probably guarding eggs, still, and didn't run fast enough."

"From what?"

Josh sighs. "Jason or a pack of juvenile rex, most likely."

Oh dear, he's right. I can just imagine Jason, furious, vindictive, driving smack through any nesting ground he comes across while chasing his missing rex, smashing eggs and mowing down would-be protective parents. And dozens of curious juvenile rex would trash a nesting ground just as fast, however hard the velociraptors fought. I guess every decision you make has unintended consequences.

Slowly, reluctantly, Josh pushes away from the rock, his body rigid with pain. I pull his arm across my shoulder again, pretending I don't hear his indrawn breath, and we go on our way. Without speaking. There's nothing to say.

We have to reach the 'Vi—or die.

DARRYL

Although I definitely feel safer in among the crags, I may have made the wrong decision leaving the valley floor. It's so *dark* up here. The moon has gone behind the clouds again. I can't see any lights out there, but I still don't trust that I'm not line of sight with Jason's camp. If he was allowing his thirst for revenge to trump his common sense, he might have switched the lights off to trick us into showing one. I don't dare use my flashlight on anything but the very lowest setting. It allows me to find my footing, but barely anything more. If I get lost out here...

That would be very, very bad. I've checked myself over by feel and I don't think I have any broken skin— no blood scent, thank God. But I'm still just one small and lightly armed human, alone in the wilderness. I need to reach the 'Vi as quickly as possible, for Harry and Josh's sake as much as my own. Until I'm back, they can't leave. And getting far away from Jason has just become a burning priority for all three of us.

That in mind, I keep going, groping and scrambling my way higher up the mountainside. I think I still know where that ridge is. Up there ahead of me. If I can get to that, follow it towards the mountain...

An eerie scream splits the darkness. I freeze, my heart rate accelerating before my mind identifies it as nothing more than the cry of a mountain fox. *Calm down, Darryl.*

I'd never heard foxes until I came to work for Josh in the 'Vi. They don't thrive in lowland areas—not enough cover—and they couldn't get inside the farm fence, anyway. I'm still not totally used to the creepy noise they make. Josh would grin if I said that.

Heck, I want to see Josh grinning at me.

Trying to breathe quietly instead of pant noisily, I haul myself up a steep part, thrusting my chest up over the top and pushing with my legs...

My hands touch...*nothing*. I flail, trying to break the momentum that's carrying me forward. My knee catches against something rough, checking my movement and allowing me to wriggle back into a more balanced position. I raise a hand to my shoulder, where I've clipped my flashlight, hesitate...then turn it up. I think I'm pointing away from Jason's camp and I need to know what I'm facing.

The beam disappears into blackness—my heart lurches. It's a deep ravine. Deep, deep, deep. And I almost toppled into it head first. I glance around. To one side is a flat area. I shift cautiously until I can climb onto it, then turn the flashlight down again and lie, breathing hard.

That was too close. Far, far too close. There's a reason why wandering around unknown mountain slopes in almost total darkness is considered insane. Eventually, I rise to my knees, looking around. I've got to keep going. How do I get around this ravine?

I glance up at the skyline, seeking my goal, but I can barely make out the shape of the mountains against the clouded night sky, it's that dark. A sickening wave of disorientation hits me. *Is* that the right peak ahead? Or is it more to the right? Have I got turned around, somehow, with all the twisting and turning?

Panting, I kneel, staring up into the darkness, my mind spinning. I'm not sure. Saint Des help me, I'm just not sure.

Eventually, I check the time. It's almost three in the morning. Even at this time of the year, it will only be a few hours before a hint of pre-dawn begins to lighten the sky. If I could see, I'm sure I'd recognize the right mountain. I'm not hopelessly lost yet—but I will be, if I keep blundering around. Despite the desperate need for speed, I've only one option. I have to den up and wait until I can see where I'm going. And I need to move as little as possible from this spot to do it, because I was confident where I was going until just recently.

Seething with frustration, I open the flashlight's aperture a fraction more and look around. There's nothing here, no crags or caves or alcoves of any kind that will help keep me warm for a few more hours of freezing darkness.

I move along the ravine edge, climb between two rocks, and find a slightly clearer area to my left. A few straggly bushes grow and...yes, that rock to the left juts out at an angle, leaving a long horizontal space underneath. It might possibly keep out a deinon, though velociraptors could definitely get under it, so it's not great. But it's right here, and there's even some foliage for scentCam.

There's not enough vegetation to cut down enough to provide any serious warmth, so I focus on masking my scent by gashing the branches I cut repeatedly with my knife and scrunching up the leaves to release as much sap as possible. I'd rather not get my rustly silver survival blanket out, because of the noise, but if I get too cold I can. My parka is top quality; Josh insisted on that when he asked Technicolor to bring winter gear for us. And I'll only be here for a few hours. If I'm a little chilly it will help prevent me from nodding off, anyway. So it's good, right?

I keep reminding myself of that as I tuck myself into the crack, pulling the last of the scentCam in after me, and lie there shivering.

Come on, sun. Rise.

HARRY

I carry on murmuring the odd remark to Josh, for distraction and encouragement—but he doesn't respond at all, except to point us in the direction we should go. He leans on me more and more, until I'm terrified he really is going to collapse.

What he said to me shortly after we set off on this endless climb is burned into my brain: *"I'm bigger than you and you can't carry me. That's just a plain fact. If it gets to the point where I can't keep going, you leave me and get yourself back to the 'Vi. That's an order. Understand?"*

Increasingly, I find myself trying to work out what to do if he does go down and stay down. If I remain with him...no one is coming to help us. Darryl hasn't a clue where we are. Jason and his guys could probably track us easily enough, but it wouldn't be help they'd bring. Despite having rejected—in my own mind—the idea of leaving him, it's clear that staying wouldn't do him any good, not in the long term. And he's right, I can't carry him. My shoulder and back ache and my legs are like lead just from supporting him this much.

I *would* have to leave him. But not permanently, the way he meant. I'd have to get back to the 'Vi as fast as I could, leave a note for Darryl, get some weapons and painkillers and medical stuff and come back to him. See if I could get him up and moving again and if not at least I'd have a chance of protecting him until Darryl followed my tracks and came to help. Yeah. It's a plan.

If...*if* I could actually find the 'Vi. I've never thought of myself as being especially bad at finding my way around but I guess growing up on a farm in one place the way Darryl and I did doesn't really let you develop your sense of direction. I know the 'Vi is somewhere up this mountain but this isn't the way we came down and it's so dark, I honestly don't have a clue where it is.

Although Josh is too tired to talk and although we keep torturously re-tracing our steps and looping around whenever we encounter something we can't climb up—which happens more and more often as Josh's strength fails—Josh seems as confident as a homing pigeon when it comes to where we're going, thank God.

If he gets too weak to route-find, Saint Des knows where we'll end up.

But he stays with it. I provide the muscle and he provides the navigation and eventually—unbelievably—we're stumbling through narrow ravines that look more and more like those where we hid the 'Vi.

Josh is so tense with pain already, it takes me a moment to realize he's gone tenser still.

"Something's stalking us," he breathes.

My heart lurches uncomfortably. "What?"

"Not mammal, so not wolves. Probably deinons."

Outage. Deinonychus stand as tall as a short woman, though thankfully at this time of year they'll only be found alone or in pairs.

"Just one?"

He shakes his head. *Darn.* Two.

"I think I can stay up if you prop me against this cliff face," he murmurs. "Flick the frights if you get a chance but, above all, make contact with that prod. I'll try and poke 'em too."

My tongue is glued to the roof of my mouth, but somehow I peel it free and say...squeak, "*'Kay.*"

With his bad shoulder resting against the rock-face, Josh breathes in borderline grunts, but he keeps moving, slowly but surely. Guess getting to the 'Vi is still our top priority. I walk beside him, prod at the ready.

Flick the frights if I have a chance.

Zap them with the prod.

Zap them with the prod. Right.

"Should I turn the flashlight up?"

"No. We'll lose all vision outside of its beam. That's dangerous."

He's right. In the dim light we can't see well, but we've got a broad field of vision. If I turn it up we'll see only one spot.

Step by step. Josh grunting softly as he rests his weight on his bad shoulder to keep his good arm free. Step by step.

Why don't they attack? Guess we must be pretty unfamiliar prey. They're cautious. That's good. If we can zap them...

Where's the 'Vi? Surely we must be nearly there?

I think I catch a slight movement from the corner of my eye, but when I swing around to point the flashlight, there's nothing there. The skin prickles coldly all up my back. Stalking us, Josh said.

Waiting for their moment.

They sure are.

DARRYL

Even with the cold and the stress I'm getting sleepy. After over a week of the three of us keeping a twenty-four hour watch on Jason as we waited for him to lead us to wherever he was keeping Dad—so much for that—I was tired enough before tonight's expedition. But I really, really ought to keep awake. Josh taught us all the survival skills and procedures. And you never sleep out-Vi unless you absolutely have to. And I don't need to. As soon as I've light to see by, I can be back at the 'Vi in an hour, allowing for the altitude gain and poor terrain. Two at very most. I need to stay awake.

Scuffing sounds pull me from...*ugh*...a doze. Something's in the clearing! A number of somethings. I lie very, very still, listening hard.

A few soft hisses and crooning sounds. My belly goes cold. Velociraptors. If it's a whole pack and they find me...

I concentrate on lying very, very still. I've got good scentCam and I'm wearing scentBlock cream anyway. Thank God I didn't get that noisy blanket out.

I listen hard, trying to differentiate where the different noises come from and estimate their numbers, the way Josh taught me. Not many...I don't think. A full pack, way out here, could be twelve or more. Sounds like six, absolute max.

I hope I'm right.

A couple are prowling around. A trace of moonlight reflects off glossy feathers as one approaches my den—I hold my breath. It sniffs around the branches, then grabs hold of one and pulls at it. Risking a tiny movement, I twist my hand and grab the branch, holding tight. *Outage,* for a creature the size of a small wolf it's strong. Fortunately, raptors have very long thin necks and compared to any wolf-shaped animal, they can't actually pull or carry much in their mouths at all.

Its strength shocks me, but I'm able to hold on.

The raptor lets go and heads along the side of my pile of scentCam. My heart's pounding so hard I'm afraid it will hear. Can it smell me?

No? It's continued past my den and is sniffing under the unoccupied part of the overhang, scratching aside a few twigs, by the sound of it. Thank God I took the time to arrange the scentCam around me properly, in a complete half moon, feet and head too, or it could just wander along under the rock and stumble over my feet.

That hint of moonlight has gone. I listen hard. The one that tried to move my branch shepherds—I think— the others to the overhang. Scuffing sounds, tails swishing, more crooning and hissing. They're settling down. Heck, they're using this place for the exact same purpose as I am, aren't they?

Will they spot me when the sun comes up? How opaque is my scentCam? I haven't a clue. I collected it in such dim light...

I don't think there are many of them, though. And I do have the electric prod. I mustn't panic. Well, Josh would say I shouldn't panic anyway. And he'd be right.

One thing's for sure, though—I really mustn't fall asleep now!

HARRY

Nothing happens. Josh shuffles and grunts. Step by step. Towards the 'Vi. Step by step.

Maybe...maybe we're *too* unfamiliar. Maybe they're not that hungry.

In winter? With snow on the ground?

But they haven't attacked yet. And surely we'll be at the 'Vi soon? The shadowy shape of these ravine walls is starting to look familiar. Yeah, we'll be there soon.

"Don't relax," Josh murmurs.

I'm not rela—

A stone shifts; movement at the corner of my eye...I spin around. A pale, feathery shape erupts from the darkness. A glimpse of teeth... No time for the frights, I barely get the prod up, clutching it with both hands... The deinon recoils, screeching in pain as the sparking tip jabs into its neck.

Movement to my left...I try to turn, but another pained screech tells me that Josh has managed to land a hit. My deinon spins around and bolts into the night— pain flares as a solid, feathery tail smacks me across the face. Blood trickles from my walloped nose as the other deinon charges after the first, but Josh has bled so much it hardly matters. Mopping my nose on my sleeve with no regard for normal scent procedures, I turn to Josh.

He's leaning, forehead to the cliff to take the weight from his shoulder, his eyes scrunched closed in agony.

Guess lunging at the critter jolted his ribs. Heck, he's tough, fighting off a deinon in this condition.

"Are you okay?"

"Yeah," he gasps. "Come on; let's try to make some speed." He reaches out, clearly wanting my support again, so I pull his arm over my shoulder. His rough breathing borders on a sob. He's not feeling good.

"We scared them off, right?" I check.

"Temporarily," he gasps. "This much blood scent, if they're hungry enough, they might have another try. The prods will have shook them up badly, though, so we should have time to get back to the 'Vi."

Well, that's something. And it sounds like the 'Vi is close. Thank God!

In fact, a few twists and turns later...there it is. Our massive, armored RV cum monster truck, with its huge wheels, high ground clearance, and full turret on top. Well, Josh's. Darryl's and my home for almost the last year, though, since we went on the run from the city-folk, who think all orphans belong in-city whether they want to go or not.

"Josh, we're here!"

No response but labored breathing. I hit the door control as soon as we reach the vehicle and the familiar hiss as it slides back is the most welcome sound I've ever heard.

"Josh, we're here. Can you climb in?"

He gets his good arm up onto the doorway but his attempt to lift himself makes him groan. He can't climb in that way.

Heck, if we get eaten at the 'Vi door I'll be so mad! Propping him against the vehicle, I drop to my hands and knees. "Climb on me, Josh. Get your feet on my shoulders."

He doesn't argue. Heck, he's heavy. Muscle. But I manage to push upwards, getting half to my feet before he finally manages to drag himself in. As I chuck the prods in and climb quickly up after him, hitting the door 'close' button, I realize that I could've just dropped the rear ramp for Josh to walk up.

Never mind. Safe. *Oh, thank you God!*

"Darryl?" I call. No answer. I didn't expect one. She'd have said something by now.

Josh still lies on the floor, groaning, but when I stand he immediately gasps, "Shutters!"

"Yeah, don't worry." I double-check all the shutters are closed before turning the lights on. Home sweet home. It feels strange, like we've been away for days, not hours. Hard to believe that we set out yesterday evening so happy and confident, hoping to find Dad down in Jason's camp. This night has been a total disaster.

Well, I guess not a total disaster. No one got shot or eaten or captured. As far as I'm aware.

Saint Des, please look after Darryl?

I can't help my big sis. I need to look after Josh.

I crouch beside him, my stomach churning uncomfortably as the light reveals just how bloody his parka and pants are. Is the bleeding really stopped?

His groans have tailed off, but he's shaking violently. Cold? Shock? Relief? All three, probably. I shuffle to the side and activate the heater, then return.

"Josh, I need to get your parka off." I touch his good shoulder hesitantly.

"Gimme...gimme a moment."

"Josh, you might still be bleeding."

"Need...need a moment..."

Maybe I should just cut it off him. That's what they do in hospital, at least in movies. And it's already got rex teeth marks in it. It is his best jacket, though. Maybe he'd rather patch it.

I remove the frights from my forearms, dumping them on the table, then open the medicine cabinet. There are some very strong painkillers in here, right? Morphine... Here. I rip off one of the individually wrapped pre-loaded syringes. Surely Josh needs it? The thought of sticking the needle in him brings me out in a cold sweat, even though I remember him saying there was nothing to it, jab it in absolutely anywhere.

"Josh, I'm gonna give you some morphine. Then I'll be able to get to your wound."

"What?" Groaning, he pushes up from the floor at last, into a sitting position against the nearest cupboard front. "No...don't give me that. It'll put me to sleep. If Jason turns up...no."

"Josh, you *need* it!"

"No. Just put it away and help me with my jacket."

Ugh. He's stubborn. And I still struggle to grasp how tough he is, even after all this time. But at least he's going to let me get to his wound now.

By the time we manage to wriggle his parka off, his brown skin has such a sickly grey-green tinge that I'm not surprised when he gasps, "Just cut the shirt."

Not such a serious loss as a top quality winter parka. I oblige, peeling it away as gently as I can to avoid jolting his broken ribs. There's the wound. Wounds. My throat tightens as I see the half circle of punctures in good light. Over his collar bone, around across his chest, the final one skewing his upper arm. And the same shape on the back. No wonder he can't seem to use that arm. Some of them *are* seeping blood, though I'm not sure if that's just because the fabric pulled clotting crystals out when it came off.

My hands shake as I put the shirt aside. I can't deal with this! If only Darryl was here. She's good at first aid. First aid? This isn't first aid, this...this is hospital-level, surely? Stitches and...stuff. Josh claimed it didn't manage to bite down, but surely he needs a scan, or something, to check for internal injuries. I mean, a *rex* bite?

"Josh..." My voice squeaks, and I clear my throat. *Stay calm, Harry, for pity's sake stay calm.* Even Josh can only take so much. "Uh, what should I do first? Stop the bleeding completely or...um...clean out the wounds?"

"Stop the bleeding," whispers Josh. "If I lose much more blood I'm gonna be flat on the floor."

And that's no good if Jason shows up, hangs in the air unsaid. Oh, hurry up, Darryl! I'm not convinced Josh could actually fire a rifle, even now, so if the worst happens, I'm going to be defending the 'Vi single-handed.

"Inject a ton of antisepsis serum around the bites," Josh instructs me. "The crystals are already antibacterial so that will be buying us some time."

I do as he says, though my hands shake so much that drawing the antisepsis serum from the bottle is difficult. My confidence improves—and my hands steady—as he fails to react to the needle pricks. Tough as rex hide. If only his *hide* was that tough, he wouldn't have got bit so bad.

When I get the odor control wipes out to start cleaning his skin, he stops me.

"Hot drink, first. Hot water...well, drinkable temperature. And then a coffee. I need liquids. Blood scent doesn't matter so much up here—won't be any rex scrambling around this high. And there's two types of antibiotics in the cupboard. Give me one of both."

Drinks and antibiotics. He's right. I should have thought of that. I hurry to the boiler tap. If only I could be as calm as Josh is. As Darryl would be. He's the one with the *short-circuiting* rex bite and he's still the one telling me what to do. I should...I should just *know*.

Frustration seethes inside me as I carry the mug to him. I've spent almost a year training as a hunter and I'm still flapping around like a pachy that's taken one too many blows to the head, forgetting everything!

I almost expect Josh to fix me with a look and a slight smile and say something perceptive and motivational to me, the way he normally does when I'm feeling this way. But he just closes his eyes, slumping against the cupboards as he greedily guzzles the warm water. His hands are shaking too.

I guess I shouldn't let the fact that he's functioning fool me. He's only just functioning. I've got to think for myself, think what to do. He might forget something, in this condition, or make a bad call. Easy-peasy. He didn't think of dropping that ramp either, and he knows this vehicle a hundred times better than I do.

Okay, Harry. Stop looking to Josh. What do you do next?

Thoughts race through my brain so fast it's almost thrumming. *No. No, calm down, Harry.* I close my eyes, take several deep breathes and force myself to slow my mind. To concentrate on one idea at a time.

If Josh needs to drink, he needs to eat. I remember from his first aid training. Sensible hunters always keep a pack of freeze-dried liver in reserve, in case of blood loss. Lots of iron in it or something. I open the freeze-drier cabinet and fish around in the corner. Yes, here it is. 'Liver' in Josh's blocky handwriting and a cross, marked in black pen but meant to symbolize the red cross on the medicine cabinet. Do not eat, in other words. Except in emergencies. We've eaten up several old packs over the year, after Josh labeled a fresh one.

I open the packet and stick the meat into the food-processor, which suggests a long re-hydration and cooking cycle that would no doubt result in deliciously tender liver, but I override several settings and it agrees to have it done in less than thirty minutes. Who cares if it's a little tough, so long as it's safe for Josh to eat ASAP?

When I turn back to Josh his head has fallen against the cabinet and my heart lurches, then I realize he's sound asleep, the empty mug toppled over on the floor. Well, there's no way I'm getting him to bed single-handed and it's cruel to wake him. His pants are so bloody, though. I fish out one of the foil survival blankets and wrap it around him instead of using his sleeping bag. The foil can go in the incinerator for sterilization and recycling, one less thing to wash. I arrange an open side towards the heater, hoping he'll warm up quicker that way.

Okay. Food's in. Josh is resting. Once he's eaten and drunk some more, I should probably clean the wounds. My gut writhes. If only Darryl would get back! She'd do a much better job. I've got about thirty minutes for other jobs.

First, I change out of my blood-stained clothing and bundle it into the washer, taking a quick shower to get rid of sweat and any traces of blood that might have made it through to my skin. That's one lot of blood scent I *can* deal with.

Should I go up the turret and keep a look-out for Jason? He can't sneak into the 'Vi, that's for sure, and with our armored shutters closed over the windows, we'd be a tough nut to crack. But I need to know if he comes, so I can drive us away before he gets to work with an oxyacetylene welder or something. The thought of having to navigate back out of these ravines without Josh's help is horrifying, but he did say he'd logged our route in on the navigation system.

I grab a coffee and a left-over rock cake from the fridge and move towards the turret ladder, my rifle over my shoulder, then hesitate. Should I wake Josh and give him a rock cake? But he's deep-asleep. Better just to leave him until the liver is ready.

I scoot up into the turret, careful the lights are off

before I raise the shutters. Far away down in the valley bottom, Jason's camp is lit up like Christmas. I put the coffee and rock cake aside and take a look through my telescopic sights. I should've brought Josh's sights up, they're better. It's normally considered very rude to touch someone else's main rifle, but in the circumstances...

The exterior floodlights are on, but there's no sign of any people. All three—four?—of them are probably out trying to round up rex and herd them back to camp. Would that even work? They've only got the one vehicle, right? Hard to herd critters that aren't used to being herded with one single vehicle. So will they be darting them and hauling them back one by one behind their 'Vi? *Fifty* juveniles? Even just trying to cull them all would be a massive operation.

I can't quite bring myself to actually *hope* that Caleb got eaten when Josh let the juvenile T. rex out to give us a chance to escape, because it would partly be our fault—but it sure would make our lives easier if Jason never found out who was responsible for this.

JOSHUA

"Josh?" Harry's voice draws me from a lovely doze, back into painful consciousness. "Josh? You need to eat this."

He doesn't shake my shoulder, thank Saint Des, and I open my eyes quickly before he can get any such idea.

He's holding out a bowl with a hunk of liver in it. I brace myself for the pain, then reach out with my good arm to take it, the silver blanket rustling loud in my ears. Liver. Blanket. He's on top of things. Good boy. His cheeks aren't as pale or his face as strained as when I dropped off. Good.

I rest the bowl in my lap and stab the liver with the fork he hands me, simply raising it to my mouth and gnawing at it. I don't crave it at all—I've no appetite—but that must be shock. I know I need to eat. My body has to put the iron and water together and make me some nice new blood.

"What's happening?" I ask Harry, in between chewing.

"Lots of lights down in the camp, but no sign of Jason or the others. Guess they're hunting for their stock." A grin peeps onto his face. "Oh, the she-rex have been wandering out of their barn and off through the hole in the fence, one by one, so I guess Jason didn't notice their pens were set to unlock. They haven't fought much, just gone their separate ways." His face falls. "No sign of Darryl yet."

My insides clench. I motivated myself a lot of the way up this mountain with the thought of getting back out there and helping Darryl. Only now do I allow myself to acknowledge what I knew deep down all along—that it's hopeless. Sure, if I were okay I could trot back down that mountain and pick up Darryl's trail. But she'd probably beat me to the 'Vi and then I'd be the one delaying everyone. And right now? I can't physically do it. I barely made it back here as it was.

Pain throbs through my shoulder and stabs my ribs with each breath. I can barely concentrate, even for something as important as this. I've broken ribs before and been bit before, but never by a rex, nothing like this.

"Josh," Harry speaks firmly, his voice only trembling slightly, "when you've eaten that and had another drink, I think I should clean your wounds."

"Yeah," I agree around another mouthful. There could be scraps of fabric from my parka or Saint Des knows what from the rex's teeth in there. It *is* urgent. I just need enough blood in me even more.

He relaxes slightly, but also looks more terrified. I wish Darryl were here and I bet he does too. How calm and competent she was, the day we met. Despite the horrible tragedy that had just struck them, she sat me down and tended my injured foot as well as any hunter-born could've done. Harry's learned well, and he is a steady boy, but he lacks her edge.

I chew away diligently, though Harry has to wake me once when I fall asleep with a piece of liver hanging out of my mouth like a dead raptor's tongue. Heck, I'm tired. But I dutifully drink two more mugs filled with thick hot chocolate. The sugar eases the last of my shocky tremor—it's Harry's hands that tremble now as he removes supplies from the medicine cupboard, lining them up on a chair beside me.

"It's fine, Harry," I manage. He's way stressed about this. "Just take each individual puncture by itself, as though each was the only one. The number of them doesn't make the slightest difference to how you clean one out."

"Yeah, okay."

I shiver as he eases the blanket away from my shoulder, still bone-chilled.

"Are you sure you don't want morphine? Anything at all?"

I don't shake my head because every tiny movement hurts too much. "No. I doubt Jason's gonna come for us straightaway. But what if he *did* decide catching the rex was a lost cause and he'd rather take revenge while he could? I'm no use to you flat out snoring."

From the anxious pinch to his face, he's not sure I'm any use to him awake, either, right now. Fair enough. But he arranges a work light and leans over the first wound without saying anything, a look of grim determination on his young face.

Fourteen. When I were fourteen my Dad got *et up*

by a rex. But hunting's a tougher life than farming and I were more mature than Harry. This is a lot for him to deal with. Though he's handled himself real well, so far. I'm proud of him.

Agh... Pain spikes as Harry eases some clotting crystals out of the first puncture with tweezers. He can't use the gentler dissolving solution because he's gonna need to get more crystals in there quick, once the wound is clean, and the solution will stop them working.

I eye my shoulder as best I can, taking stock of the punctures. Too many... "Most of those will need a staple or two."

"Right." He wriggles a small surgical clamp into the hole with trembling fingers and cranks it open a little, rinsing the wound out with the water syringe and peering inside it. *Ow. Ow. Ow.*

"It's bleeding again." He sounds discouraged. "I can't really see."

"You need to just flush it out real well and then stop the bleeding again. Can't do more than that with a wound this fresh."

"How do we know if there's...if there's worse damage, Josh?"

I have a crystal-clear memory of that rex's teeth sliding through my skin, my prod activating in its mouth a split second later, its mouth flying wide as it recoils. No feeling or sound of crunching and only a hint of pressure. "It didn't bite down, Harry. The only other damage is the broken ribs, from when I fell off." And they're almost certainly just cracked, not broken. No jagged edges sticking into my lungs, anyway, or I'd be coughing blood by now. "Honestly, none of it is as bad as it looks."

I hope I'm not lying through my teeth, but it's not like there's a *misfiring* thing we can do about it.

Sorry, Saint Des. You know I do try not to swear. But I'm finding it a little hard, tonight.

HARRY

I set the final staple in the final puncture wound, my shoulders aching from bending over so tensely for so long. I'm going to suggest we get Josh's bloody pants off, but he sorta gently topples over onto his good side, with a soft groan, controlling his descent slightly with his good arm, and falls sound asleep. Or passes out. I'm not really sure how to tell.

I check the time. Heck, we've been at it for almost two hours. No wonder he's exhausted. The pain must've been excruciating. The pants will have to wait. It may go against normal procedure but Josh is right. A rex large enough to breach the 'Vi won't climb this high and spinos never venture far from large bodies of water.

Scientists still argue whether they count as land or aquatic 'saurs.

Carefully, I tuck the thermal blanket back over him; try to wriggle it under him to protect him from the cold metal floor, then tidy away all the medical supplies. I really hope the wounds are clean. I did the best I could.

Now, if only Darryl would turn up, we could get out of here.

I make a sandwich and climb back up the turret. Jason's camp still glows with light. No one in sight. Even the she-rex are all gone. I sit, and eat, and watch, checking all around, checking the thermal scans. Even though Josh is asleep just below, I feel horribly alone in the darkness. Not that I would put it past Josh to leap up and fight if Jason did arrive, but...I don't know. He might be too weak.

I feel almightily responsible right now, anyway. For everything. And however much I may have complained when Josh or Darryl occasionally treated me like a child, having everything depend on you is not as fun as I would've thought.

DARRYL

The sky is definitely lightening. I can make out the peaks clearly against the sky, now. I'd be pleased, except for the heap of sleeping velociraptors lying near my feet. I can't see them yet, tucked in the shadows under the overhang. Hopefully they can't see me either.

From the soft breathing sounds in the night silence, they *are* sleeping. Should I try to sneak away before it gets light? No, between the crunching of snow in the drifts and the scuffing of rock on the wind-swept areas, they'll hear the moment I move. I need to stay still and quiet and hope they leave without noticing me.

My hand is aching again. For the hundredth time I try to relax my grip on the electric prod. I hope it will be enough to fight them off with, but it's dodgy. If they manage to pull me down, get a three-inch claw in my belly... I appreciate raptors more after this year out in the wilds, learning about them from Josh—as a farmer I just hated them for what they sometimes did to our young stock—but I don't underestimate how dangerous they are, even small ones like these.

I occupy myself with another silent Chaplet of Saint Desmond, for Harry and Josh as well as for me. At least Harry's with Josh. I hope he is...

Jesus, I trust in you...

The sky has lightened still further by the time I finish. Individual rocks in the clearing are visible, now, the curve of snowdrifts, the bushes poking up in between...

Near my feet, a raptor stretches and yawns. *Uh-oh.* No, not *uh-oh.* The sooner they go, the less chance they'll see me in the dim light.

The raptor's up, prowling the clearing, sniffing around. Small, his dapple-grey velociraptor plumage still showing juvenile patterning, his ruff lacking its full adult coloring. One of last year's chicks. When it starts to climb the further slope, another raptor bounces from beneath the rock, snarling. A glossy adult male. His ruff is almost jet black, a less common coloring and very striking.

Chastened, the juvenile returns to the others. The big male runs around, doing what I'm pretty sure is a dawn security sweep, before returning as well. He doesn't notice me, lying here in the darkness under the rock. Was it him yanking on my scentCam earlier? His ruff feathers are certainly glossy enough.

Soon the raptors are all up. They stretch, then sit around and preen themselves as diligently as any cats. Hoping to avoid notice from larger predators—just the same as me.

Four. Two adults, two juveniles. I finally get an accurate count. My stomach unknots a little. Facing four velociraptors with nothing but a stick would be an uncomfortable confrontation for someone my size, though not hopeless, but with the prod, the odds are very high that I can scare them off. If I have to.

What the...?

A little bundle of feathers has just dropped from the

back of the adult female, rolled onto its feet and started toddling around. In the most adorable way. It's a chick, and a young one. Definitely only a hatchling not a nestling, probably very new-hatched indeed from the look of its fluffy clumsy tinyness. Four more plop from the mother and start to explore under her weary watch, though one tires almost immediately and gets tucked up under her breast feathers. The male settles beside her to preen her and be preened in return, and he watches alertly as well. A mated pair, clearly.

Why the heck are they roaming around these mountains with their new-hatched chicks? Something must have happened to their nesting ground—there should be more pack members than this.

I frown. Hmm. Juvenile rex, maybe? Oh dear.

Actually...I've been so stunned by the cuteness of the chicks that only belatedly do the implications sink in. *Hatchlings*. If they think I'm threatening the hatchlings...

Oh boy. I need to lie really, *really* still.

JOSHUA

I'm woken by Harry trying to get me to eat more liver and have another drink. He's right, but I want to snarl at him to leave me the heck alone. I was having such a nice sleep. Being awake *hurts*.

I manage to bite my tongue and accept the liver with some hint of gratitude. Harry reports that the sky is lightening. Good. If Darryl had to stop to wait for light, she'll be moving again now.

As long as she's okay. What if she hurt herself falling from the rex, just like I did? What if she's been lying out there in the snow all these hours? What if Jason and his guys found her?

"I'm wondering—" says Harry.

"No," I say.

"You don't know what I was going to say!"

"You were gonna suggest you go look for Darryl. No. You're not an experienced enough tracker. And even if I were fit to go, I'd still give it at least one more hour. It won't help if she gets back here and one of us is off out there instead. Weigh the odds."

Harry subsides, his expression see-sawing between sullen and relieved. He must be worried sick about his sis. Well, so am I, but it don't change the facts. First, we have to give Darryl a chance to find her own way back.

We left behind anything that could give feedback squeals and give us away, like ScreamerBands and earpieces, but she'd have to be so close to the 'Vi to connect to those she'd be almost back anyway. We just have to wait a little longer.

"Can you pass me my handPad?"

When Harry does, I get up a map of the surrounding terrain and study it, though my brain feels like it's stuffed with tar-sodden cotton balls.

"Okay," I say at last. "If she ain't back in a few hours time, our best bet is to drive through the area she probably ended up in. Try to attract her attention."

"What about Jason?" Harry's eyes dart nervously towards the wall in the camp direction.

"I don't mean let off flares. Just rev the engine some and wait around. Find open areas to drive through, where we can be seen. It's still risky, but I don't see what else we can do. You can't track her and I can't track her, if for different reasons."

Harry's face falls and he stares at the floor. He probably feels I'm being hard on him.

"Harry, the wind's risen, hasn't it?" I can hear it, whistling around the turret.

He nods anyway.

"A lot of tracks will have been blown away. And the snow is patchy up here, lots of areas of bare rock—no tracks. You're a real good tracker for someone who only started learning seriously less than a year ago. But you can't track an hours-old trail over this terrain and in these conditions. It's just a fact. You'd get lost yourself, like as not, and then we'd be worse off than before."

He nods, silently, and thrusts the hot drink out. I accept it, but I still feel bad. I *have* hurt his feelings.

"Harry, I'm real glad you were with me tonight. I

wouldn't have got back up that mountain without you and you've done a great job on my shoulder and everything. Thank you."

He stands a little straighter and shoots me an 'aw-shucks-don't-mention-it' sorta smile. That's better. Now, let's see if I can empty this mug before I flop again.

DARRYL

After leaving the clearing for a while, the adult male returns from a successful hunt. He has blood around his mouth, anyway. When he drops his muzzle to them, the chicks lick eagerly at his jaw, until he heaves up a mess of softened and partially digested meat. Probably an unlucky rabbit. A single velociraptor can't hunt anything much bigger than that, this quickly. Wearing down larger prey with multiple slashes from their killing claws takes time.

The juveniles draw nearer, eyeing the food, but the female snarls, driving them away as the chicks feed hungrily. Well, except the small, weak one. That one manages only a few mouthfuls, then slumps beside the mother again.

When the others have finished, the mother and father eat the rest, the female taking most. Whether she was the pack matriarch before, she is now, and female raptors wear the pants. The two juveniles whine and squirm but get ignored. The new chicks come first and, in their interests, the parents come second. No doubt as soon as they find a replacement den site, the male and at least one of the juveniles will go to hunt something bigger, while the female — larger and more dangerous than the male — and the other juvenile stay to guard the chicks. Or maybe both juveniles will go hunting. With so few pack members, the balance between protecting the hatchlings and hunting effectively will be difficult.

This overhang doesn't provide good enough shelter for a permanent den, though. They'll want somewhere far more defensible now there are so few of them. So they'll be leaving now. *Please, Saint Des?*

After another quick preen to get rid of any traces of blood, they are getting to their feet, the matriarch calling authoritatively. One of the chicks, invigorated by its meal, toddles determinedly towards me, regardless. *No! Go away...*

It tugs at the branches with tiny teeth, maybe smelling its father's saliva.

Go *away*.

I can see awfully well through my shielding vegetation and it's getting so light now I don't trust that —

The male approaches, grabbing his naughty chick in his mouth and popping it onto his back. He swings his head around again...then goes motionless, his eyes staring...into mine?

His head lowers, his shoulders hunching, ruff flaring. His long feathered tail sweeps up, swishing behind him, taking up space to make him look bigger. Body language that could signal the beginning of either defensiveness or aggression.

He sees me, doesn't he? He sees *something* is under here. And from flat on the ground, he looks enormous!

He snarls a warning and the matriarch grabs chicks and tosses them onto her back, poised in a moment to run. They're nervous after whatever has happened to them. Lucky for me.

The male still stands, though, staring under the rock as he tries to make out what I am. Danger...or food? I poke the tip of the prod out and activate it. *Zap-crackle.* Blue sparks leap between the prongs and he springs back, hissing in alarm. With Jason's fence in the area, he must know what electricity is.

A sharp call from him and the matriarch flees with the juveniles at her heels. He backs up slowly, then flicks around and bolts after them, his two little feet with their great killing claws pattering through the snow as his tail swishes the air behind.

And then there's nothing but a little churned-up snowdust floating down to settle over the footprints. I let out a long breath, limp as a wilted lettuce leaf.

They're gone.

HARRY

Josh is sound asleep again. Still slumped on the living area floor in his gory pants. He must be exhausted. I'll have to wake him soon. It's been almost two hours and there's still no sign of Darryl.

Jason's 'Vi drove back into the camp once, towing an unconscious rex. One of the juveniles, from the small size. He and another guy got down from the 'Vi and went into the egg barn, came out again, waved their hands a lot and probably turned the air blue, so he knows he's lost his she-rex, now, too. They've driven away again, but the memory makes me shiver. I didn't need to hear what they were saying to know how mad they were.

A movement to the left draws my eyes. Relief hits like a full-force blow to my sternum. Darryl is hurrying towards the 'Vi, prod in hand, her eyes darting around warily as she watches for danger. She looks furtive, but perfectly okay.

Opening the side door from the turret console, I just manage to make myself stay put to provide cover. As soon as the door hisses shut below, I close the polarized windows to keep the light from showing before yanking the hatch up. By the time I've reached the bottom of the ladder Darryl's just clambering to her feet, looking stiff and tired.

"Darryl!" I lunge for her, but my sternum gets a

blow for real when she thrusts her hand out to stop me.

"Careful! Not too tight."

My heart plummets. "Oh no, you're hurt as well?"

"No, I'm fine. What do you mean, *as well*?" Despite her words, she gives me an oddly gentle hug and draws away quickly before I can lose control and crush her to me.

"Josh got bit by a rex." I point to him lying there on the floor, sleeping through all our noise, and her breath catches, face tensing in horror.

"*Bit* by... How bad—?"

"He says it's not too bad. Flesh wounds. But there's so *many* of them... And he broke some ribs falling."

"*Outage.*" Darryl hurries to crouch beside Josh, lifting the foil blanket and wincing as she sees all the stapled wounds in his shoulder. I slathered them with antiseptic but haven't put liquid skin on yet. When you see it as one massive bite, not lots of little wounds the way Josh has been encouraging me to, it looks horrendous.

"Did you clean them out?"

"Yes, I did my very best. He *said* I did it well." I can't keep the uncertainty from my voice, because we both know Josh might've said that just to be encouraging.

"Good. We should get him clean and in bed properly."

"Yeah, good luck with that. Until we're away from here, anyway."

"Good point. We need to go. He put the route in the nav system; we don't need to wake him."

"Oh, come on, he'll want to know you're safe. He can have another drink, anyway. He's got a lot of blood to replace."

"How did you even get back up here with him in that state?"

I grunt an almost-laugh. "Walked, obviously. It was a real fun trip."

"I bet." She eyes Josh again, then calls gently, "Josh? *Josh?*"

It takes a gentle prod to his good shoulder before he groans and opens his eyes. But the relief and joy that flare in them gives me a slight lump in my throat.

"*Darryl!*"

"Hiya. Sorry it took me so long. I almost fell down a chasm and nearly got lost so I had to stop and wait for daylight. Then a pack of velociraptors decided to curl up near my feet and I had to wait for them to leave. And then—"

"It doesn't matter, you're back!" Josh grins, bleary but delighted.

I go to make him another coffee. When I turn back to them, Darryl has unzipped her parka and is carefully lifting something out. What?

I go closer, peering at the tiny thing cupped in her hands. Is that a *chick*?

"I'd never have brought it back if I knew things were this serious here," she says. "But this was the weak one. I was going the same way as the pack to start with—what was left of the pack—and I could see from the tracks that it kept falling off. And then, there it was, lying there in the snow. I guess eventually they gave up and left it."

"When it couldn't hang on any more." Josh nods. "They couldn't carry it in their mouth for long, the way a wolf would, so at that point they'd leave it and save the others. Don't worry, Darryl, of course you had to bring it back. Let's see..."

Of course, grunting in pain, Josh is struggling up into a sitting position and reaching out his good hand for the tiny ball of feathers. He couldn't get up to change his pants, but for a critter in distress...

"What is it?" I ask, still not managing to get a clear look, it's so small.

"Velociraptor," Darryl says.

"Not one of the ones we saw?" I say to Josh.

"Almost certainly." He sits it in his lap and examines it with his good hand. "Well, there's nothing obviously wrong with it. It's just very small. Probably struggled to stay warm as they travelled. Normally at this age it would be tucked under its mother's or father's breast most of the time, not being carted around on their back, exposed to the elements. He seems pretty warm now, I guess because you had him in your jacket, Darryl."

"Good. I'll drive, we'd better get going."

Yeah, we definitely need to get out of here!

"Feed the chick first," says Josh. "At this age, if we don't get some food into it, it will probably die. There's liver ready cooked. If Harry pulverizes a little, it should be able to eat it. Won't take long, then Harry can put it in his parka while we travel."

My heart rises a little, at that. I get to look after the critter? Cool. I hand Darryl Josh's coffee and hurry to mash some liver.

"What are we going to do with it if it survives?" I can't help asking.

"Pass it to Technicolor to sell to a zoo. Or at this age maybe to a petting farm as a no-touching exhibit and they'll sell it on when it's grown-up. Except..." Josh frowns.

Except, if we're fleeing the state, we won't be seeing Technicolor for who knows how long.

"Or sell it direct to a zoo in Yoming, I guess," he adds. "Or wherever we go."

A frown flits across Darryl's face, too. 'Cos I don't see what we can do, now, other than leave Exception State, put plenty of distance between us and Jason, but it means giving up on Dad *and* making things worse for Josh, legally speaking. The authorities claim he 'kidnapped' us just because he was eighteen when we joined him and we weren't—and apparently crossing state lines makes it even worse.

Heck, this has not gone the way we hoped.

Darryl doesn't say anything. After making Josh lean forward so she can inspect the wounds on his back, she leaves him to drink his coffee and goes to make herself one, slurping at it while assembling a sandwich one-handed. Oops, I should have got her something already, she must be famished, thirsty, and cold.

Too late now. Once I have a little dish of soft liver paste I take it over to Josh. The chick lies in his lap, asleep.

"Come here, tiny fellow." I pick the chick up, making it give the teeny-weeniest peep of protest. "*Heck*, he's cute."

Josh gives a very tired smirk over his coffee but apparently doesn't have the energy to say 'I told you so.'

I put the chick's mouth to the paste and, after a puzzled sniff, it starts eating.

"That's right, tiny guy. Eat up."

"It seems early for chicks to be hatched," says Darryl. "I'd have thought they'd only just be laying, at this altitude."

"I'm sure their nesting ground was sited near an abandoned building," says Josh.

"Huh? What difference does that make?"

He sips again before answering. "You know a lot of out-of-the-way buildings had installed those deep-sunk thermal heat generators before the Rewilding happened? And after people abandoned those properties a lot of the pipes burst open, making those hot springs that are fun to swim in?"

We both nod because we've visited several since coming to work for him, so he goes on, "It's not that uncommon for carni'saurs to make nests near 'em—s'why this ain't the time of year for hot spring swimming. Sometimes it works to their benefit, allowing their chicks to hatch the moment food supplies are increasing with spring and give 'em the longest possible time to grow before the next winter. Sometimes it works against 'em, though, if the warmth tricks 'em and they lay and hatch the chicks too early—I've seen that happen. These ones timed it fairly well."

"They've still got four chicks," Darryl says. "And both parents survived."

The chick's stopped eating already so I fetch a teaspoon as Josh says, "Well, that ain't too bad. Hopefully the others will be okay."

"Come on, Tiny, eat a little more," I urge the chick, putting a spoonful to his mouth.

"We're selling it," says Josh, in a very firm voice. "It *can't* be a pet."

"I know that!" Illegal, domesticating any kind of raptor. And stupid-dangerous, if it's not imprinted on you. Good, Tiny's accepting the food, now he doesn't have to dip his head to take it.

"It can be easy to get too attached, when it's this little and helpless," Josh persists.

He's probably right. But... "He still needs a name, right?"

Josh gives a faint smile and says nothing more. Either too tired or thinking if I get too fond it will be a good learning experience for me or something.

I'm not going to get too fond. I'm not a fool. Doesn't mean I can't enjoy having the little critter around for a while! Judging by the way Darryl's eyes are darting between Josh and the cab and the handPad she's commandeered off him, my big sis will be too busy being the uninjured, responsible adult—or almost-adult, in city-folk eyes—to worry about Tiny, even if she was the one to find him. She can deal with angry Jason, injured Josh, and the rabid city-folk—I'll just raise the chick.

After the night I've had, this division of responsibilities is fine by me!

DARRYL

My mind tries to dart in a dozen different directions, calculating, wondering. We're all exhausted and we need to sleep, but we also need to get far away from here. We hid the 'Vi very carefully, though, so can we get far enough away to be safe before we simply have to stop and rest, or would we be better snatching a few Zs here first?

"What's Jason doing?" I ask. "Any idea?"

"Appears to be looking for rex," says Harry. "Except I've only seen him bring one back. I guess he could be looking for his intruders and he just happened upon that one. No way to be sure."

Hmm. If Harry had seen him bringing back a rex every hour, maybe getting some sleep would have been best. But in this case...

"I think we should get under way. Josh, we need to get you blood-free." There'll be large carni'saurs around, once we get lower down, large enough to open up the 'Vi and eat us.

He sits up straighter, wincing only slightly. "Yeah, no worries. Harry, can you grab me some clean stuff from the cab as soon as you're done? I'll need to shower."

Harry shoots Josh a surprised look, though I'm not sure why, then goes back to coaxing meat down the chick. He's clearly keen to take responsibility for 'Tiny,' which I'm glad of, considering how he felt about raptors when we first came to work for Josh. And I've got enough to worry about.

Speaking of...I open the critter cage and peep in. Kiko's asleep. Easy to forget how early it still is. I leave the cage open so the little 'quadravian' can come out when he wakes up and realizes we're back. I left him a ton of food and water in the hope he'd be okay if we got caught and it took Jason a long time to find the HabVi. Jason wouldn't have been likely to hurt Kiko; microraptors are too valuable in the pet trade.

"Harry," I say, "if you're nearly done, I'll go up the turret while Josh gets clean."

"Okay."

I reach for Josh's telescopic sights and give him an inquiring look. He nods, so I unhook them and turn towards the turret.

Someone needs to keep an eye on Jason.

JOSHUA

I am *so* glad Darryl is back safely. But now that gut-twisting anxiety has eased, a deeper fear turns my insides into an echoing void. Darryl won't tamely follow my lead, the way Harry does. I *have* to be okay. I have to *seem* okay. If I don't, she's gonna start using the H word. And that's the same thing as the P word, for me.

I *ain't* going to prison. I ain't. Being in-city is enough to give wilderness-raised me a panic-attack. To be *locked up* in there, helpless, month after month, year after year, unable to escape...

Cold sweat breaks out on my forehead and the void in my belly turns into a howling vortex.

I'm *fine*. I'm gonna be fine. I just have to make her believe it.

Setting my jaw against the pain, I make sure to haul myself to my feet before she's reached the top of the ladder, so she sees me stand by myself. I do feel much stronger, after the food and the liquid and the sleep. Comparatively. I'm gonna tire easily for weeks, of course, after losing that much blood. But the worst of the immediate ill-effects are easing. The pain is un-dimmed, but the fear makes it easier to ignore.

Harry gives me an awed look as he comes out of my little cab bedroom with the clean clothes he's just collected from my drawers.

"Told you it looked worse than it is," I say calmly, wishing Darryl could hear, but of course she's closed the hatch behind her. "Blood loss was the worst thing."

I have to let him help me, since I've only one good hand and I need to keep the bite as dry as possible, but before long I'm clean and dry, the wound's been painted with liquid skin, and I'm in fresh clothes—and feeling like a wrung-out dishcloth after all the exertion.

"You can let Darryl know we're ready to go," I tell Harry, refusing to allow the exhaustion into my voice.

"Okay!" Looking a thousand times happier now I'm up and acting normal and his sis is back and he has a new not-pet, Harry scoots up the ladder to the turret so energetically it draws a weak smile to my lips.

But I'm alone...for a moment. I move quickly to the medicine cupboard, open it, and grab a strip of the morphine injections, slipping it into my pocket. I add a couple of blister packs of more normal painkillers and one of emergency stimulant pills, then close the cupboard again. I've just time to get into the cab and transfer the stash into the little private cupboard by the head end of my seat-bed—the one neither of them would open—get it closed and lower myself onto the seat, before Darryl enters.

DARRYL

"Harry's clearing the decks for travel," I tell Josh, as I settle into the driver's seat and reattach the sights to his rifle, which he or Harry has moved to its usual travelling position between the seats. "We can be off in a minute. Where are we going?"

Clean and dressed normally, the alarming wound hidden under a shirt and his second best parka, he looks much better. But his brown skin remains tinged grayish with fatigue and his stiff posture betrays how much pain he's in.

"Away from here, first of all. It's gonna take us a while to reach another state. Spring melt is coming — you can smell it. It was starting when we left the lowlands. There'll be mud everywhere, thawing lakes and marshes, swollen watercourses. You and Harry simply aren't experienced enough to drive the 'Vi over some terrain, in this weather. If we can get far enough away from here to be safe, we may just have to wait awhile, until I heal up."

If he's totally discounting the possibility of him driving any time soon, he must be feeling bad.

A slight frown creases his brow, though, and he mutters, "Or...mebbe we should keep going, even if it's slow...in the circumstances."

Meaning, we'd have to reach another state before he could safely go in-city to a hospital? Yeah, he's right. We need to keep heading for the border as fast as we can, just in case.

Besides... "What are the odds of Jason catching us if we're too slow leaving Exception?"

He smiles, to hear me mention 'odds' like a proper hunter, I guess. "In the short-term, low, as long as he doesn't pick up our tracks leaving here. But we've got the brushes fixed behind the rear wheels and the wind or the melt will get rid of any remaining traces fast enough. Since we won't be going near a 'Vi-park, he's got no way to find us. Long-term, there's too much chance of running into him to stick around. You heard him—shoot on sight—and that was before he knew it was *me*."

"Yeah, I get that. We have to go. That was our one and only lead on Dad, anyway. At this point I know he'd want us to save ourselves."

"Seeing that he's probably dead anyway." Josh winces and shoots me a look, a hint of color finally entering his cheeks. "I'm real sorry, I shouldn't'a..."

"No, it's true." Okay, he was blunt, but I guess no one's at their most tactful after being chomped on by a T. rex.

I eye him again as Harry finally calls down on the intercom that he's up in the turret, ready to keep watch as we travel.

"You sure you don't want to lie down on the seat, Josh, sleep while we go?"

He shakes his head firmly. "This terrain up here *definitely* counts as unsuitable for you to be driving on. I at least need to be able to give you tips. If we had any other choice..." He twists his lip and says nothing more.

If we had any other choice, he wouldn't be risking his precious 'Vi on these slidey, snowy slopes in my inexperienced hands, right. Fair enough. Apparently in *his* hands would be even more of a risk, right now. Since I'm sure I remember him telling us about a long journey he once drove regardless of cracked ribs...yeah, he really doesn't feel good.

I run through the departure sequence, raising the stabilizers and opening the cab shutters, then turn the key. The engine purrs into life and soon we're creeping through the ravines. The console screen helpfully shows the route we came in by, imposed over the map. But like many hunters, Josh only bothers to capture really complicated routes, relying on memory elsewhere.

So, yeah, actually, I do need him awake, even leaving the driving aside.

JOSHUA

After two hours of bracing myself as the 'Vi lurches, tilts, bumps, and slides over the torturous mountain terrain, my ribs and shoulder burn so badly that my head's spinning. I can't lean back without stabs of agony, but if I sit forward I sway—agonizingly. I try to keep smiling, but even that's starting to take too much energy—though every time Darryl shoots me an anxious look a stab of fear gives me a shot of adrenalin and helps me do a little better.

By the time she pulls to a halt for a comfort break I can barely wait for her to leave the cab before yanking that cupboard open and pulling out a morphine syringe. Ripping open the packaging, I stick the needle straight through my pants, forcing myself to inject only a quarter of its contents. I just need to stop her getting too worried...

Capping the needle again, I replace it in the cupboard, close it carefully, then lean against my good side, waiting for the stuff to kick in.

Ah...a little of the pain is melting away, already. That's real nice. Mebbe I can bear a few more hours of motion, after all. I was about ready to beg her to *stop, just stop, just stop*—despite how important it may be for us—me, especially—to reach the border with all speed.

I don't want to be too obvious so rather than look super-perky all of a sudden I rest my cheek on the seat back and pretend to be dozing...

Huh? Oh, Darryl's offering me a mug. My doze became real. I smile a thank-you as I take it, careful not to make it *too* chirpy.

She gives me a firm look over the top of her own mug. "We need to keep a close eye on that shoulder of yours."

"Sure do," I say calmly, even approvingly. "But they *are* flesh wounds and with the antibiotics—it should be fine."

"Animal bites and scratches often get infected."

"Sure do," I say again. "That's why we carry the

antibiotics, y'know."

She looks reassured, so I guess I didn't emphasize enough in my training that virtually no antibiotics in pill-form are guaranteed to be a match for twenty-five punctures from a carni'saur's filthy teeth, wounds that went almost three hours before being cleaned. Which is a right good thing, in the circumstances.

"Harry okay?" I ask, sipping my coffee.

"Sure. Tired, obviously. But he's keeping alert up there. At least, when Tiny's asleep and not distracting him. He's feeding him now."

"I heard that," comes Harry's voice, from the living area.

Darryl grins.

DARRYL

I peer through the windshield, fighting to stay alert. When we finally made it down from the mountains onto easier terrain, I was able to allow Harry to drive while I slept for a few hours. Yeah, so no one was keeping watch, but it allowed us to keep moving. Then Harry—who had a far worse night than I did, by the sound of it—couldn't keep his eyes open, so I'm driving again while he sleeps.

I shoot a look at Josh. Even knowing how tough he is, I'm surprised how well he's bearing the travel. Harry said he completely refused painkillers, just like when we first met him and he had that nasty wound in his foot. Doesn't want to be drowsy if anything kicks off.

Despite that, after hours of travel and with less need for input from him on this easier terrain, his head has finally sunk against the seat and he's asleep. Which I'm glad to see because the motion of the vehicle must be incredibly painful for him. If I can just manage not to drive us into any concealed mud...

Ugh, *my* head's nodding too. I jerk it up again. The sun hangs low in the sky. Somehow, incredibly, we've managed to keep going for the whole day. We're going to have to stop soon, though. I should look out for a safe, discreet spot.

Even with the conditions—the snow *is* melting down here, big time—and the earlier mountain terrain, and my inexperience, we've covered a good amount of ground. No distance at all compared to driving on the highway, of course, but still—no way Jason will be anywhere near here, tracking his rex. Only reason he'd come this far would be if he was tracking *us*.

Harry and I will need to split the night watch between us for a few days, until we're sure we've left Jason behind. It's going to be grueling—but it's better than getting caught. Jason was prepared to kill us simply because we'd *seen* his lucrative illegal operation. Now that we've effectively destroyed it and he may even know it was Josh that did it...

Yeah, it's worth losing some sleep to stay out of his hands.

JOSHUA

Dimly, I'm aware of the 'Vi drawing to a halt, the engine cutting off, the familiar sound and motion of the stabilizers going down. I guess we're stopped for the night. Darryl slips through into the living area without speaking to me, closing the door behind her. Trying to let me sleep.

I open my eyes and push myself forward off the seat-back, trying to smother my gasps as pain slashes through my chest. The broken ribs hurt the most, but it's the bite that's most dangerous. My final quarter of morphine is wearing off, big time. Still, the syringeful has allowed me to get through the day without coming across as too desperately unwell. I mean, I'm *not* too desperately unwell, really. It just hurts so much it might come *across* that way and I can't risk that.

I lean forward slowly and check the map on the dash console. We've made good time considering the inexperienced drivers, but it's a tiny fraction of the distance to the nearest state border. I glance out the window at the twilit landscape. Melting snow. The conditions are only gonna get worse over the next few days. We're unable to go onto a highway without the cameras picking up our plates and the very smallest, quietest minor roads—the ones we might actually consider driving on—will be turning into rivers of mud. We'll be off-road the entire way. It's gonna take over a week to reach Yoming.

I touch my bitten shoulder cautiously, then regret it as pain spikes. A week. *Misfire*, a wound like this, it's all gonna be settled, one way or another, well before then. Maybe I'll be fine. But no matter what, I've gotta carry on *seeming* fine just as long as possible. It's my only chance.

I open my little cupboard. I've gotta seem like I'm bouncing back from the blood loss. Reassure them both, real well.

Saint Des, please help?

HARRY

"Okay, the food's ready," says Darryl, snatching me from a doze. "Can you wake Josh?"

"Sure." I take Tiny from my lap and tuck him gently back inside my parka—he's sooooo cute—then drag myself up from the chair I sat down in after setting the table.

I tap on the cab door, then open it. Josh is lying down, sleeping. "Josh? Food's ready."

"Hmm?" He stirs and raises his head. "Oh, thanks. I sure am ready for something."

He sits up, very carefully, but he's moving much easier than earlier. Darryl said he managed to sleep for much of the afternoon; it must've done him a lot of good.

He sits in a chair immediately when he gets to the table, without offering to help, but he'd hardly dare do otherwise in his condition, with Darryl there.

"Want to cuddle Tiny?" I offer, reaching into my parka, confident of his response.

He hesitates a fraction, though, before smiling and holding out his good hand. Guess he is still feeling pretty tired. But he settles Tiny on his lap, stroking him gently.

"Have you seen his *claws*?" I say. "If I'd got a look at those I'd never have had to ask *what he was*. I didn't realize they hatched out with them so large."

"They hatch with 'em in proportion," Josh says. "It ain't really that odd."

"Something that cute with a pair of those things; it is!"

Josh laughs softly.

"Sorry to break up the raptor appreciation party," says Darryl, also smiling as she plunks the foodProcessor's big dish on the table. "Let's eat."

"Amen," I say.

"I haven't said grace yet," says Darryl.

"Wasn't that it?" I tease. "Well, hurry up!"

We had a sandwich lunch but being so wide-awake and active for the entire of last night, to say nothing of being out in the cold, has left us very hungry. I think technically it's Josh's turn to say grace, but since he's, what's it, *convalescing* Darryl clearly feels she should do it.

"Dear Lord, thank you for food and thank you for our escape from Camp Jason," she says. "We pray for Josh's speedy recovery and that you watch over us on this journey. Amen." She looks towards the gun cabinet, inside which our little home tabernacle nestles safely, and crosses herself. "Oh, and if Jason could fail to re-capture many of those poor abused rex," she adds.

"Amen," I say, crossing myself too.

"Amen," murmurs Josh, eyes down as he still strokes Tiny, though he breaks off to glance and cross himself as well.

Now we can eat.

DARRYL

It's such a relief that Josh is able to sit at the table normally and eat with us. When I got back to the 'Vi this morning and he was lying there all blood-stained on the floor, wrapped in that blanket, I really feared the worst. I guess he lost a lot of blood, but his body must be well on the way to replacing it all, now. All the same, we need to keep a close eye on that bite. I dread to think what we'll do if it gets infected. We're so far from the border.

Speaking of which...I get up and cross to the medicine cabinet, come back with two pills. "Antibiotics, Josh."

"Thanks." He swallows them down with a swig of water.

So that's another dose into him. He's had four, now. Good.

I make some hot drinks and we sit slowly sipping, watching Tiny toddling around the tabletop licking at our empty plates while Kiko hunches on my shoulder, staring suspiciously at the itsy-bitsy predator. Even Harry's quiet; we're all tired. Eventually, the console pings and Josh very slowly, very carefully leans to check the screen.

"Message from Technicolor."

"Everything okay?"

"Yeah, fine. They've taken a juicy contract culling allos in the north-east. But they'll be back within the month to resupply us, they say. Well, imply."

Most of our communications with Technicolor are semi-coded, through allusions and pre-arranged phrases—since the city-folk are still proactively hunting for us. Fernanda 'Frilly' Matthews, that vile investigator from the CPS, keeps interviewing West, Thiago, Ed, Uncle Mau, Father Ben, and absolutely anyone she can connect to us or Josh. No one's sure what lengths she's allowed to go to and whether it includes hacking our messaging accounts.

"Guess we'll have to let them know somehow that we're leaving," Josh goes on. "I'll try to draft something tomorrow."

He sounds sad, and I know how he feels. We won't be hunted anymore, in Yoming—murder is the only real extraditable crime nowadays and Josh hasn't killed anyone—but we'll be leaving everything we know behind—including our good friends in Technicolor 'Vi. Without them, we'd have been caught months ago—or had to leave. We'll miss West's wedding, no doubt—but at least he'll feel free to propose to Trudi once we're gone.

"We need to bear in mind what Uncle Mau said," Harry remarks.

Our neighbor, Maurice, who would've been our guardian if Dad hadn't messed up the paperwork and caused this whole mess by landing the state in that role instead, told Father Ben that he'd been checking up about our legal situation if we crossed the border. He confirmed that Yoming wouldn't be interested in us but said that if Exception was bothered enough, they could apply for special federal permission to come get us themselves.

"Surely even Fernanda wouldn't go that far?" I say, though I'm trying to convince myself as much as anyone else. The woman seems obsessed.

"We can make very quick supply trips in-city," says Harry eagerly. "Very, very quick. In and out. Different city each time. They'll always be one step behind. Or we don't stay in Yoming, we just *keep going*. There's a load of states out there! I bet I'd be eighteen by the time we'd travelled around every one, and then we could come home to the farm!"

There's an idea we hadn't really thought of. Hunters tend to learn an area and stick within it, mostly. Local knowledge makes life unSPARKed safer. But Harry's idea has a certain attraction—and it would foil Fernanda Matthews!

I don't know how I feel about returning to the farm anymore, though. The hunting was only supposed to be temporary, to stay free until we rescued Dad. But I really love this life. The wildlife, the wilderness. The realness of it all. Yeah, it's tough, but it makes me feel very free and alive. I guess I'm glad Harry's so keen to go back to the farm. It's not fair to expect our neighbors to run it for us forever, even if they are getting compensated. A Franklyn should run it and, if Harry's offering, maybe that's a good thing.

"And Josh can consider our farm as his home camp, like, forever, right?" Harry burbles on, picking Tiny up again.

Josh raises his head as though he was almost dozing, but smiles. I guess he appreciates the thought, because he forebears to point out that he doesn't want a camp! Dark smudgy circles ring his eyes. He should probably turn in. And either Harry or I need to get up that turret and keep watch, and the other to bed. We don't want to waste a minute of daylight getting to that border, with its safe hospitals beyond, and that means we both need to be as well-rested as possible so one of us can be driving at all times.

Maybe Harry sees the thought in my eyes— anyway, he empties his mug with one last long swig and tucks Tiny inside his parka. "I guess I'd better go on watch first," he says glumly. "Since you did most of the driving today."

"Thanks, Harry," I say. 'Cause he's right, and I'll probably end up doing more of the driving tomorrow, too, if the conditions stay like this.

Up he goes, murmuring something to Tiny. The chick is already getting stronger. He's so small, it's easy to imitate the life he'd be living back in the nest— spending most of the day snug and warm under his parents' feathers, with occasional explorations of the nest environment and regular meals. When he grows he'll have to go into the critter cage, of course. Raptors do make deceptively affectionate, intelligent pets—but lacking millennia of domestication, they also attack un-imprinted-upon humans about fifty to a hundred times more often than pet dogs, even people who've raised them from Tiny's age. No secret why they're illegal.

Josh sits droopily, like he hopes the last few sips of his tea will give him the energy to get up and head to bed, so I don't nag him to go.

"What do you think of Harry's idea of touring all the states?" I ask instead.

Josh raises his head tiredly and smiles—equally tiredly. "I like it. A lotta hunters do it, y'know, just once. Especially just after they've managed to club together and buy their own 'Vi."

"It does sound like a great way to fill in the time until Harry and I are free of Fernanda's well-meaning manhunt."

Josh bares his teeth as though laughing but doesn't actually, probably to spare his ribs. "*Well-meaning.* That's generous of you."

I make a face. "I do get that she thinks she's doing the right thing. She's just...just so clueless."

"City-folk," sniffs Josh, drinking the last of his tea. He sets the mug on the table. "Well, I'm turning in."

"Good. You sleep hard and get better."

"Do my best."

He eases to his feet and disappears into the cab. Doesn't he need to use the head? Oh well, he sure knows where it is, he's lived in this vehicle since it replaced their old one when he was eight.

Time for *my* bed, too.

JOSHUA

A feeling that I need to do something important tugs at me as I drift up from a deep sleep. I check the time. I've slept for several hours. Is Harry still on watch?

I feel my bitten shoulder with my good hand. Hot. Guess it would be a miracle if it didn't grow *at all* hot. I'll get up and take some more antibiotics. Daytime-only doses ain't enough, for this. If anything will be. And mebbe I can talk to Harry. That's important. Could be important. I can still hope.

First, I fish a fresh morphine syringe from the cupboard and give myself a small dose. But when I try to sit up, my head swims. I feel weak as a...as Tiny, left lying in the snow to die. Mebbe I should've rested, instead of getting up to eat dinner with them. But it sure did a good job of reassuring Darryl. But now I feel almost as weak as when Harry and I made it back to the 'Vi.

Yep, I'm gonna come across like a dying dog. No good. I take one of the stimulants and a couple of the regular pain pills, hoping I can manage a conversation with Harry before they put me back to sleep.

I have to wait a few minutes for them to kick in and the delay chaffs at me. I need to deal with Harry now, while I can. If things get worse, it'll be hard enough to handle Darryl as it is.

Finally, I feel strong enough to push myself to my feet. A pause to wait for my head to stop spinning and I shuffle into the living room.

"Harry, I'm just taking my antibiotics," I say softly, holding down the intercom button for the turret. "Want a coffee?" He'll have to come down to get it; he knows I can't carry it up there.

"Sure, thanks."

Got'ya.

Tricking them both like this makes me feel sick and awful inside—but the thought of prison is even worse.

I swallow the antibiotics and make sure to be leaning casually against the wall, looking as healthy as I possibly can, when Harry comes down for his coffee.

Now, if I can just manage not to be too obvious about this... I don't reckon this would work with Darryl, but Harry's younger and not as sharp—but he ain't stupid, by a long shot.

Saint Des, guide my tongue. You must understand how I feel. You hated life in-city too.

DARRYL

Harry reports that Josh got up to take more antibiotics less than an hour ago and seemed even better than at dinner-time, so I resist the urge to peep into the cab and check on him. I might wake him up. He seems to be doing really well, yet every time I think about that awful wound I get anxious all over again.

I try to push the feeling away. He's on a dual-course of strong antibiotics—types city-folk would need a prescription for, though hunters can buy them under license—he's recovering quickly and we're heading for Yoming as fast as we can. There's no point stressing out. I settle in the turret with a coffee and scan the night darkness for any sign of Jason.

Josh will be fine.

We'll be in Yoming soon, free at last.

We'll spend the next three and a half years on a grand tour of the States, then Harry can take over the farm and I can decide what I want to do—or maybe I can even get custody of Harry sooner.

Everything's looking about as good as it can do, considering that we've finally had to accept Dad's loss. So why am I gripped by such a horrible sense of foreboding?

I *must* keep an eye on that wound.

And drive really fast.

JOSHUA

The pain wakes me as the small dose of morphine wears off. I've had another couple of hours' sleep, but my head is stuffed with tar again. My limbs weigh a ton each. That stimulant shouldn't have worn off yet, but I'm more exhausted than before I took it.

Weakly, I push aside my sleeping bag and clumsily unfasten the top few buttons of my shirt to take a look at my shoulder. Yep, deep, angry red surrounds at least two of the punctures. Any more detail is hidden by the blurring effect of the artificial skin and I've no idea what my back looks like. But if that ain't blood poisoning, it will be soon. I'm probably a goner.

Well, what did I expect? Most hunters, after an injury like this, would be being driven flat-out towards the nearest hospital by their anxious 'Vi-mates to be hooked up on intravenous antibiotics, pronto. Guess mine trust me a little too much. Luckily for me. That sick, guilty feeling twists my stomach again, but the fear pushes it away.

I've gotta keep this from Darryl as long as possible. So long as neither of them find out until it's too late, I'll be safe. *Right, Saint Des?*

Fumbling, I manage to do the buttons up again. I'm not making it that easy for her. I give myself another small dose of morphine to help me sleep, though I'm so fumble-fingered it's difficult. Then I lie, staring up at the shadows the bedside light casts on the ceiling.

Is Darryl asleep up there or is she up in the turret now? She's probably in the turret. I'm so sorry to abandon them like this. What will they *do*?

They could take the 'Vi and do that tour, as planned, but it won't be very safe, they ain't experienced enough. And neither of them are eighteen, to deal with the city-folk along the way. Ain't named as my heirs on my will and won't legally own the 'Vi, neither, though I don't think West would challenge them for possession of it.

Or they could give up and surrender to Fernanda.

What sort of choice is that?

But what can I do? If it's my time, it's my time. Probably is. My shoulder burns. Is that morphine ever gonna kick in? My head aches more and more. I *am* disappointed. Real disappointed. I hoped for more. A lot more. I wanted...wanted many things. But Dad hoped to bounce my kids on his knee. Uncle Z still dreamed of finding some nice lady to marry. No one gets to choose their time. And what I've had...it's been pretty darn good. I've had a wonderful life. Yeah, I'd rather go thankful, than whining.

Sure would be nice to see Dad... Uncle Z...

Mebbe I can ride the infection out, anyway. Ain't totally impossible. Heck, I'm so *tired*. Why don't I drop off to sleep again? My shoulder hurts so much...

I grope in my private cupboard and pull out Dad's rosary. Make sure to tuck it carefully out of sight inside my sleeping bag before starting a chaplet.

O Lord, you know of what we are made, dust and clay.

Our days are like grass, we bloom like a flower in the meadow;

the wind blows and we are gone…

"You've double-checked all your harness, Josh?"

"Sure have!"

"Good."

Although I'm eight, now, Dad picks me up bodily and puts me in the saddle. Marta bobs her head, excited by all the noise and activity around her, despite the blindfold, so I hold the reins firmly. The allo teeth Uncle Z threaded on strands of beads for me dangle on either side of her bridle, looking great. I can't believe I'm riding my own orni in a real race at long last! I don't even care if I come in last!

"Okay, your race is up," says Dad, as the announcer begins another call. "Just remember, riding like a man is better than winning. Anyone starts any dirty tricks, just ignore them."

"I will!"

"Though that critter will be worth a lot more if you place," mutters Uncle Z.

"Not helpful," says Dad.

"Ah, he's only gonna listen to you, anyway."

They exchange a brotherly elbow jab or two, then Dad whips the blindfold off Marta. "There we go, girl. You take care of him, now. Whoa, what the— Marta?"

With a violent twist, she throws me to the ground. Dad yells out as I get to my knees. I look up and freeze in horror. Marta, suddenly taller than Dad and with a mouthful of horrible teeth, has grabbed Dad, she's...she's eating *him!*

"No!" But in a few gulps, Dad's gone. Uncle Z dashes forward, trying to stop her—but Marta gulps him down as well.

"No! NO, Marta, stop!"

Darryl's there, grabbing for her bridle, Harry rushing in as well. NO! Marta eats them, too...

No! But it's no good. She's turning on me, she's coming, her mouth is so large, her teeth...

Pain sears as blackness surrounds me. There's nothing except pain. Except...red light. I'm standing on a...a massive stalagmite. The smooth, slippery tip is hard to balance on. Marble? A marble stalagmite. Must be a mile high. There's nothing around me, nothing at all.

"Dad? Uncle Z?" Where are they? How do I get off this thing? I can barely keep my footing...but how could I ever get off this, ever? What's down there? It looks like...lava? I'm so hot, yet my skin crawls with dread.

"Darryl? Harry?" Why would they leave me here, like this? All alone...

"Dad?"

I wake with a jolt—argh, that hurt. The smell of my own sweat fills my nose. Dampness slides slickly over my skin. I'm so *hot*. What a horrible dream. It still burns in my mind. Was it the morphine? But I didn't have that much.

Oh, God help me, it hurts. I'll have to take some more, nightmare or no nightmare. How can I smile and pretend to be okay when I feel like this? I don't try to look at my shoulder again. It's too exhausting and what does it matter? I don't need to see it, not now.

I grope in the cupboard, but my hands have been replaced with clumsy sausages that don't want to grip anything. Finally I get the syringe out. Is it the one I was...was what? What am I doing? Something important...I think. Was it? I'm so tired. Something falls from my hand onto the floor but... *Hurts*. Tired...

So hot...

DARRYL

I wake early but can't settle off again. I guess by the time I've had a bite to eat and a cup of coffee it will be almost light enough to be underway. I might as well get up.

Harry had about three hours sleep then went on watch again. We both know it's the most sensible division—more watch for him, more driving for me—

but I still felt a little bad going back to bed and leaving him yawning up there. Can't be helped. Weigh the odds, as Josh keeps drilling into us. And they're better with me well rested to drive for longer. I had three years more driving experience with farm vehicles even before Josh's lessons.

I dress and climb down into the living area, Kiko fluttering down to roost companionably on a chairback, though he promptly goes back to sleep. I make a coffee straightaway, but then I stare at the cab door, undecided. If I go in there I'll almost certainly wake Josh, and what he probably needs most is rest. But it's been hours since I saw that wound. I clearly remember him telling us—and I think I remember Dad telling us, come to that—how quickly infections can sometimes set in.

You have to be alert. That's what they both said.

Yeah. *Sorry, Josh*. The need to check is like fire-ants crawling over my skin. I don't tap on the door—better not to wake him if I can avoid it—but simply press the 'open' button. I've never known him to lock it, though he says his Uncle Z always kept that door locked at night ever since little Josh—

As I step into the little room, *not-rightness* assaults me, hard. A smell in the air—sweat and something else I don't recognize, but it raises my hackles and brings that foreboding washing back.

Josh's built-in bedside light is on but turned down low. He's lying on his back, but I can't see much more than that, except that his skin glistens oddly. I swipe the main light on. Sweat. He's soaked in it. *Oh no...*

I hurry forward, my foot knocking something on the floor. What...? Is this one of the morphine syringes? It's out of the wrapper and part-used. Josh has been taking morphine? Since when?

He hasn't reacted to the light, so I place the syringe on the dash tray and lay the back of my hand on his forehead. His skin *burns*, making me yank my hand away. Stomach cold with dread, I unfasten a couple of buttons and pull his sweat-soaked shirt to the side.

Oh God. Help us.

His shoulder's a fiery red, dark streaks radiating from at least two of the punctures. It's infected, all right.

How long has he been feeling bad? Why didn't he *tell* us? Why does he even have morphine in here, anyway?

I grab the door to Josh's private cupboard and pull it open. An empty morphine syringe... A strip of full ones in their wrappers. Blister packs of pills... *Outage,* what's he been taking? How long?

He handled the travelling yesterday so well. Getting better all day? Or merely *seeming* to get better? I remember his dark-circled eyes at dinner. *Misfire,* he's played us, hasn't he?

"Josh?" No response. Okay, we've no choice. He has to get to a hospital as fast as possible.

I bend over the dash console, calling up the map. Closest city is...Exception. The state's capital, good hospitals there, but... *Outage*, five hours, at least, even if we use the main highway. I glance at Josh as he shifts restlessly in his sleep, muttering something incomprehensible. Can he survive five hours? But that's the closest hospital; it's his only chance. I plunk myself in the driver's seat and reach for the keys. My hand closes on empty air. What the—? I check the floor. They're not there.

Josh always leaves the keys in, for safety. Pretty much all hunters do, in case a quick getaway is needed.

Unless a getaway is precisely what they wish to avoid. *Short-circuiting fences!* My growing suspicion becomes certainty. Josh has had only one goal since he got bitten, hasn't he? To avoid the hospital, no matter what the cost. How did I not anticipate that?

I kinda did. I knew he'd freak out if I had to suggest it, so I hoped I wouldn't have to, thought I'd cross that bridge only if we came to it. But he was one step ahead of me, burning the bridge down.

"*Josh!*" I crouch beside him and raise my voice. "Josh!" I shake his good shoulder, hard. "Wake up and give me the keys!"

Groaning, he drags his eyes open. They're glazed

with pain and fever, his face grey, his dark hair plastered across his forehead. "*Wha...?*"

"The *keys*, Josh. The keys to the 'Vi. I need them. Where are they?"

His eyes grow a fraction sharper as he wakes up fully. "You can't have them," he mumbles.

"I have to get you to a hospital, Josh! Give them to me *right now!*"

"Uh-uh," he snarls, fear turning his face feral. "*My* 'Vi. We go where *I* say. Not hospital. Never."

It is his 'Vi, but... "You've *got* to get to the hospital, Josh. You're gonna die!"

"Fine by me."

I jerk in a pained breath but he turns his face slightly to the side, avoiding my eyes, staring at the cupboards as though looking through them to our little tabernacle on the other side of the wall. I've a feeling he's thinking, though, fever-slow, so I stay quiet for a while.

"Josh..." I say at last.

He looks at me again and the ferocity in his eyes has shifted to desperation. "Father Ben."

"Father Ben?"

"He has what I need."

"He does?"

"Yes. I saw it."

Saw it? Father Ben does carry medicines to deliver

to the people he visits. Mostly things people need regularly. Could he have something that will help Josh?

"Josh," I say gently, "Father Ben's probably further away than the nearest hospital. I don't think that's going to work."

"He ain't. Check his schedule. He ain't that far. Shouldn't be. If you take me to Father Ben and promise not to take me in-city or...or go on the highway or...or turn me in, I'll give you the keys."

"Josh!" His demand appalls me.

"I want Father Ben! Not the hospital."

"I can't promise that, not when you're this sick..."

"Fine, no keys. Leave me alone, I'm tired." He tilts his head to the side and closes his eyes. *Outage*, he looks terrible.

But he might actually be falling asleep. What if I can't wake him again? Where would he have put the keys? Maybe they're just in his sleeping bag. No, that's too obvious. He'll have put them somewhere else and he knows every inch and crevice of this vehicle.

Frantically, I turn back to the console and swipe through the files, hunting. Here, Father Ben's latest schedule that he wrote out for us. What date is it? After the chaos of the last thirty-eight hours, I'm not even sure. I check the corner of the dash console. Okay, so...he should be...going to Kenning Farm...so...closest place to intercept would be at this minor road, just after he turns off the main highway. Less than three hours. He *is* close. Josh is right.

We'd have to hurry to have a good chance of getting there before him. But we could make it. And if he doesn't have what Josh thinks he has? I double-check the map. Yes, we'll be significantly closer to Exception City. Not an entire three hours closer because it's off at a slight angle. But significantly close. But the only way to get the keys quickly—and maybe at all—is to promise Josh... Fine, if Father Ben is a bust, *Harry* can drive us in-city.

"Josh..." He doesn't stir. I have to shake his shoulder again, making him whimper. The sound ties my stomach in a knot. "*Sorry*, Josh. Listen, I'll take you to Father Ben, okay? Please give me the keys."

He opens his eyes and blinks blurrily at me. Blankly. Slowly, memory filters back onto his face. "Promise?"

"Yes."

"*Promise?*"

Heck, he's gonna make me say it, isn't he? "I promise I will take you to Father Ben and I will not take you in-city, and I will not take you on the highway, and I will not turn you in. Okay?"

Relief spreads across his face and his whole body relaxes. He smiles at me so *trustingly,* wrenching my innards again. Then he gropes feebly at the place where the back of the seat meets the...seat of the seat. Then makes a face.

"I can't...they're down there."

"Here?" I try to cram my hand in where he indicated. *Outage*, it's tight. I would *never* have thought of looking here. *I'm* struggling to get my hand in, though it's much smaller than his.

Where...hah! I touch the keyring. With a little more painfully tight wriggling, I get it out. "Thank you, Josh." I'm not sure if he hears. He's almost asleep again. Right. I need to get Harry down here to look after Josh and I need to gets us mov—

I turn around—Harry stands in the doorway, face pale, staring at Josh, at me.

"Is he...okay?"

I swallow. "No. The wound's infected. I'm taking him to Father Ben. He says Father Ben has something that will help. Stronger antibiotics maybe. And if he hasn't..." I shoot a glance at Josh. He looks asleep—or unconscious—but I step closer to Harry and lower my voice. "If he hasn't, you'll have to drive us to the hospital because he wouldn't give me the keys unless I promised I wouldn't."

Harry's face actually pales even more. "Darryl, he— Last night, he—"

A cold prickle runs down my spine. "He, what?"

"He made me promise...it was all so light-hearted.

He said something like, *you'd* never take me in-city and turn me in, would you, Harry? It was so *light-hearted* and he seemed so *well*. And of course I said no, and he laughed and said *promise?* And I...I promised. But then...well, he looked me in the eyes kinda funny and said, 'A man always keeps his word, Harry. Remember that.'"

The blood in my veins runs ice-cold. Josh hasn't burned *a* bridge, he's been creeping around methodically torching every single bridge that could *possibly* lead to the hospital, hasn't he? And we didn't realize. He's the experienced one, our boss, always so calm, so sensible, so in-control. We didn't suspect a thing.

I should've remembered what Father Ben said, when we met him the time before last, when I got talking with him about Josh's fear of the city somehow and Josh had gone up the turret to check it was clear for Father Ben to return to his van.

"Darryl, don't you understand what a phobia is?"

"Sure. It's a fear."

"No. It's an irrational *fear. Fear of being eaten by raptors if I break down is simply a fear. The fear that would make me* choose *being eaten by raptors rather than simply climbing into that tiny dark refuge in the bottom of my van for an hour or two and surviving to live out the rest of my days, that* would be a phobia. That's what Josh has. When you and Harry make decisions about Fernanda and everything,*

just remember: Josh isn't capable of making rational decisions when the city is involved. He simply isn't."

Heck, why didn't I think things through? The only way Josh could avoid having to go to a hospital—and therefore prison—before we reached the border was to either not get sick—or to simply let himself die. I should've realized he'd go to *any* lengths to seem well.

Too late now. I settle in the driver's seat and slip the keys into the ignition. Josh saw something in Father Ben's van that will help. Unless...unless this is just another clever misdirection. Another distraction. Another time-waster, ticking his life way.

No. Josh carried a big hunk of Edmo haunch out to Father Ben's van for him the last time we met, to take to the soup kitchen since he was on his way in-city. And they were in there for a while, talking. About Josh's religious education, or lack thereof, he said, and Father Ben gave him a little tour, too. He had plenty of time to see what sorts of things Father Ben had in there. He didn't *need* to distract me, he could've just left me to hunt and hunt for the keys until he was safely dead from the fever.

Father Ben's got what Josh needs. We've just got to get to him in time.

I start the engine. "Harry, get cold water and cloths and try to cool Josh down. Give him some of the morphine from the syringe as well, try to ease the pain.

And get him to sip water as often as you can." As I pull away, I add, "Stick some more antisepsis serum in all around the wound as well, I guess." Much good that will do, now.

As the slushy landscape rolls past I fix my eyes firmly on the terrain ahead, watching for the slightest sign of mud deep enough to bog in. If we bog down, Josh will die. We haven't time to do a recovery and still intercept Father Ben.

I watch the ground ahead, watch and watch, trying to quiet the little voice in my head as again and again I see Josh's trusting smile.

If Father Ben can't help, that little voice whispers, *what do you do? Break your word—or let him die?*

HARRY

I bathe Josh's forehead with melting snow—though Darryl barely wanted to stop even long enough for me to bring in a big tubful—but he's just so hot. I lay more over his limbs, trying to wet his clothes and use them as damp clothes. Still he burns.

Once, he retches, making a stinking mess on the cab floor. Silently, I clean it up, my hands shaking. I'd clean up vomit for a month if he'd just...just...

...just *not die.* I don't like to think the word, even in my head.

He's restless, twisting and turning, though it makes him whimper in pain. He talks and cries out, speaking to his Dad, his uncle, to us, sometimes just babbling incomprehensively, though none of it makes much sense. Guess he's delirious. I give him the last of the morphine from that syringe, hoping to ease his suffering, and he sinks into a fractionally calmer sleep.

Soon he's shivering, though, shivering and shivering. "Momma," he begs, "Momma, I'm so cold. Please swaddle me, please..."

Josh never had a Mom. He must be dreaming. I pile sleeping bags over him and turn the heater up, trying to warm him. All too soon he's burning up again and I have to throw everything back through into the living room, startling Kiko. Now and then he gets a little more with it, asking for Father Ben. I tell him Father Ben will be here very soon.

"*Are* we nearly there?" I can't hold the question back any longer.

"We're not doing badly." Darryl speaks tensely, not taking her eyes from the route ahead.

"Is he" —I can't hold this back any more either, though my voice goes right up to a tiny squeak—"is he gonna be okay?"

Darryl stares fixedly through the windshield.

She doesn't answer.

I dip the cloth in the snowmelt again and lay it on

Josh's forehead. My eyes blur and tears run down my cheeks. I need to feed Tiny soon.

Why didn't Darryl answer?

But that, of course, is a what's-it-called, a rhetorical question. I'm fourteen, not four.

I start a chaplet in my head, but I keep losing my place. Never mind.

Jesus, I trust in You. Jesus, I trust in You. Please look after Josh. Please...

DARRYL

"Is he...is he gonna be okay?" Harry squeaked.

I didn't look at him. Couldn't bear to see his wide eyes and strained face; couldn't bear to take my eyes from the terrain and risk losing a second. I knew I needed to answer, say something, comfort him. But my mind was blank. Every moment Josh thrashes and mumbles and burns, it's harder and harder to believe that he's going to be okay.

Harry says the dark streaks have spread halfway across Josh's chest. *Oh God, please, please, please let him be okay...*

I drive. And drive. Try to think about nothing else. Speed. Speed. Safe speed. We mustn't bog. Speed...

A chime from the Nav system snaps my concentration. Thank God, we're nearly there. If we go around this hill, we can come up on the minor road a bare half-mile from the highway, the closest we can possibly intercept Father Ben without venturing onto the monitored road itself. Which I can't, thanks to the promise Josh wrung from me.

Unless I break it...

No need, we'd barely reach Father Ben any sooner. We'll just wait here for him.

I pull to a halt behind a good-sized hillock. The turret should have a clear view over it to the minor road, but we won't show up much. As soon as we see the SOS van approaching, we can call Father Ben on the Intercar and get him to come around to us. It's less than a quarter-mile off-road, a well-drained stretch; his van should be okay.

"You feed Tiny," I tell Harry. "I'll go up the turret until you're done, then I'll look after Josh."

"Don't you need a break? You just drove for, like, almost three hours and the conditions are—"

"I'm fine." My voice comes out sharper than I intend as I head through into the living area.

Harry nods—I'm already climbing up the ladder. I can hear his voice quivering as he talks to Tiny. Kiko is avoiding the cab, either sensing the tension or frightened by Josh's babbling, but he swoops into the turret to join me. I stroke him as I watch the road as hard as I watched the terrain while driving. We must not miss Father Ben.

Kiko wraps his tail around my neck and cuddles up to me, clearly stressed. Only Tiny is too young and innocent to pick up on the atmosphere. A horrible surge of anger at my pet sweeps me. I want to push him away, stop him from bothering me. *What does Kiko matter when Josh is lying there, like...*

With an almost physical effort, I swallow the hateful feelings down and concentrate on soothing the little quadravian. Sure, he's not Josh, but he's a living creature, with feelings, and he's done absolutely nothing wrong. Getting angry with him is totally unacceptable.

By the time Harry comes up to take over the watch, Kiko seems calmer, but I leave him with Harry rather than take him into the sick room and stress him out again.

I'm glad to be back in here with Josh. I didn't like leaving him. I take the cloth from his forehead, stroke his sodden hair back, dip the cloth and lay it in place again. His temperature remains so high. How long can a person survive this sort of fever?

Peeling his damp shirt back, I check the wound and shudder. The dark streaks snake right across his chest. We haven't even seen what his back might look like. Whatever Father Ben's carrying, it had better be good. Could he even have some sort of intravenous set-up?

But who would need that in a home setting? But Josh saw *something*.

Josh is growing more and more restless again. He keeps crying out to his Dad, to his Uncle Z, to me and to Harry, not to leave him. I stroke his hair and try to soothe him, tell him we're not going to leave him, he's safe, he's fine, but he remains terribly agitated. When he's not begging us to stay with him, he's begging for Father Ben.

"Soon, Josh," I whisper. "Very soon."

HARRY

That sight of that little black van in the distance fills me with more relief than I've felt in my life. As it gets closer, I make out the white dorsal stripe running from the front bumper over the back to the rear bumper. It's definitely Father Ben's van.

The road isn't visible for a great distance, so he's already in range. I hit the Intercar button.

"Father Ben, come around behind the hillock to your left. Ground's solid. We need you!"

"Harry? What are you guys doing here? Are you all okay?"

"Josh is hurt. Please hurry."

I focus more on scanning the landscape, now I don't need to watch the road so closely. No sign of danger.

Nothing on the heat sensors. Should be safe enough for Father Ben to leap out and into the 'Vi, even if we haven't been monitoring for long.

Father Ben doesn't waste time with more questions, concentrating on driving. His van can't deal with off-road terrain anything like the 'Vi can, so it's a much more delicate operation. But he pulls up beside us without bogging down anywhere.

"Clear?" he asks.

"Clear." I open the side door.

He leaps out with a bag in each hand. Medical supplies? And priestly ones too, I guess. The vehicle tilts a fraction as he scrambles in. I close the door and leap for the ladder.

Father Ben's here. Surely Josh will be okay?

DARRYL

My heart leaps when I hear Harry hailing Father Ben. We didn't miss him! Thank God. I'm hovering in the cab doorway when Father Ben finally climbs up into the 'Vi.

"Father Ben, it's Josh! He got bit by a rex and it's infected. So badly."

Father Ben's eyes widen in horror. "A *rex*? Why didn't you take him to the hospital?"

"He pretended he was fine and then— Never mind,

he said you had what he needed! What antibiotics do you have? Anything intravenous?"

"*Intravenous*? I don't have any antibiotics at all. I mostly carry insulin, warfarin, statins, that kind of thing."

"What?" A wave of horror washes through me. *Was this just a distraction?* "But he said he *saw* it! In your van, I presumed..."

Father Ben's face creases in confusion. "I have no idea... Is he lucid?"

"A little. Occasionally."

"Then we'd better ask him." Father Ben follows me quickly into the cab, slides past me and kneels beside the bed. "Josh?"

I lean over him to poke Josh's good shoulder gently, as Harry lurks in the doorway. "Josh? Father Ben's here?

Father Ben touches Josh's forehead, hisses in dismay, then pulls his shirt aside. His dark skin takes on a decided green tinge as the blood rushes from his face. "God above, that's bad..." he whispers. "Darryl, he needs the hospital."

"He was so sure you had what he needed..."

"I don't think I've got *anything* that can help *this*..."

"*Father Ben...*" Josh's voice is a rasp, his good hand creeping out, grabbing weakly at him. "Father Ben..."

"It's okay, Josh, I'm here." Father Ben grips his

hand firmly, talking very slowly and clearly. "Now, Darryl says I've got something you need. What is it?"

"Bap...tize me. Need...baptize me. Want...Dad... Uncle Z...Darryl...H...H..." He trails off, panting.

This time the wave of horror is so strong my head buzzes and echoes and I slump to my knees, afraid I'm going to pass out. It's not medicine. It was *never* medicine that he wanted.

"Baptize..." Father Ben shoots me a puzzled look. "I thought he was baptized already?"

Somehow I shake free of my shock and dismay enough to reply. "He is. His dad did it, he said. But when he was five his dad got worried whether he did it right and tried to get a priest to do it. The priest freaked out about Josh living unSPARKed and tried to take him, made such a scene they ran away and never went near a church again."

Father Ben winces, but I add, "He said his dad read up about it some more and decided he had done it right and stopped worrying. But I know Josh has a really clear memory of the grown-ups fighting over him in the church parking lot, so I guess that's what's in his head, right now."

"I see. That makes sense." Father Ben squeezes Josh's hand gently, drawing one of his two bags towards him with the other. "It's okay, Josh, I can do that right now. Don't you worry."

"Father Ben!" I protest. "He's already baptized! This is *not* the most important thing right now!"

Father Ben takes a bottle of holy water from the bag and looks me in the eyes, his face more serious than I've ever seen it. "Darryl, the state he's in, a conditional baptism *is* the very most important thing right now. If there's a shadow of doubt...and for his peace of mind."

I shudder, wrapping my arms around my chest, trying to hold myself together. I want to weep. I want to *scream*. Josh can't die. He can't. *Oh God, please!*

In the doorway, Harry makes a sniffling sound. I ought to go and hug him, but I can't seem to move.

Father Ben is already pouring the holy water onto Josh's forehead, once, twice, thrice, saying softly, "Joshua Wilson, if you are not yet baptized, I baptize you in the name of the Father, and of the Son, and of the Holy Spirit. Amen." He traces a cross on Josh's forehead, then strokes his head gently. "There, Joshua. It's all done. Nothing to worry about."

Josh gives a vague smile, like he only half-remembers what's going on, but when he turns his face away and closes his eyes and sinks away from consciousness again he seems considerably less agitated all of a sudden. How long I've wished he could rest so peacefully—but now it terrifies me.

I displace Father Ben in the position closest to Josh, seizing his hand, stroking his burning cheek. "Josh, please fight," I whisper. "You've got to fight. Please? Please keep fighting..."

But he doesn't want to fight, does he? He wants to flee. Flee to his dad, to his uncle, flee from the city... Now he's sure he'll reach them, he's not going to fight any more, is he? Talking to him won't help. The only thing that will help...

"*Fight, Josh!*" I kiss his cheek, then rise. "Harry, will you look after Josh?"

I take Father Ben into the living area, where there's more room for us both. "He needs proper medical care," I say, "but he maneuvered both of us into promising not to take him in-city or on the highway and now I don't know what to do!"

Father Ben sniffs. "I'm honestly not sure a promise in these circumstances should be considered binding."

Again I see that trusting way Josh looked at me. I get what Father Ben means, but it sure *feels* binding...

"It doesn't matter now," Father Ben says firmly. "*You* promised. I didn't."

He turns towards the cab, his attention set on the driver's seat, and my heart leaps and lurches all at once. If I don't try to stop Father Ben...will Josh consider this a betrayal? But he didn't make me to promise not to let *someone else* take him to the city.

Anyway, who *cares* if he's angry with me — if he's alive to be!

Harry looks around, eyes widening with relief and hope. But we're still several hours from Exception City. By the time we get there, will they still be able to help Josh? Will he even be alive? A heavy HabVi is a go-anywhere vehicle, not a go-fast vehicle. Should we try to transfer Josh to Father's Ben's van? In fact...

"Wait! Father Ben, if we take him in *your* van, not only will it be faster, but we can hide him in the refuge to get him through the city gates. Harry and I are underage, we don't need ID cards. We take him to the hospital, I bet they'll get busy treating him right away, the state he's in, no time for questions, then as soon as he's stabilized we sneak him off again before they figure out who he is. What do you think?"

Father Ben grimaces, as though it's all somewhat more evasion of the law than he's really comfortable with.

"*Please*, Father Ben?" begs Harry, seeing his reluctance.

"They'll send him to *prison*, Father Ben," I say. "And it ain't exaggeration to say that he'd rather die!"

His face softens. "Alright, alright. I know he's only ever tried to help you two—I don't want to see him go to prison, either. And both options involve me being found in you guys' company, so what the heck, we'll give it a try. But it's a long shot, okay?"

Yeah, I know that. But at least it's a shot *and* we'll

get him there quicker. My heart lifts and I follow Father Ben into the cab, though there's barely any space. How will we move Josh? A movement catches my eye through the windshield—before I can look, a voice blares from the Intercar so loud and sudden shock jolts every muscle in my body.

"HABITAT VEHICLE, YOU ARE SURROUNDED. PUT DOWN YOUR WEAPONS, OPEN THE DOORS AND PREPARE TO BE BOARDED."

HARRY

A highway patrol truck has just pulled right across our nose! Darryl dives out of the cab, lunging for the console, using both hands to access the camera feeds and press the button to close the cab shutters, all at once. *Snick.*

I squeeze past Father Ben and look over her shoulder at the screen. *Outage,* there's another highway patrol vehicle pulled smack up against our rear bumper, blocking us from moving, and out-city police cars sit at a distance on each side, with officers pointing assault rifles from behind the grilled windows.

"We're surrounded..." Darryl whispers.

I stare at the screen. "*How* are they here?"

Father Ben turns toward the side door, outside which his van is parked, his face twisting in dismay.

"They must've slipped a tracker in my van! I told you Ms. Matthews was getting too interested in me."

Outage. In our worry for Josh, we totally forgot we were supposed to be cautious about meeting Father Ben.

"But here so *quickly*?" whispers Darryl.

"There's an emergency services dispatch hub at the nearest SPARKed rest area on the highway," Father Ben adds grimly. "Less than two miles away. Moment my tracker went off-road, they must've sent them from there."

My heart pounds, sweat soaking me. They've found us. What do we do? I stare at Darryl, who stares at the console, her face white, her eyes fixed. Okay, so we were willing to go onto a highway and drive up to the city-gates to save Josh—effectively handing ourselves over to the city-folk. But we'd just figured out a way around that...

The voice booms from our Intercar again.

"HABITAT VEHICLE, YOU ARE SURROUNDED. PUT DOWN YOUR WEAPONS, OPEN THE DOORS AND PREPARE TO BE BOARDED."

"Why did you close the shutters, Darryl?" Father Ben speaks in a very steady voice. "We have to let them in. There's nothing else we can do."

Darryl remains motionless. Her rifle's leaning against the console and her hand's gripping its strap, tight. Somehow, trying to get Josh to the hospital and...*letting them in*, giving ourselves up, *right here*...seem very different.

"Darryl, any resistance at this point will only make things worse," Father Ben persists. "And they'll get Josh in-city far faster in an ambulance than we can with our cloak and dagger plan. This might just be the thing that saves his life."

Darryl draws a deep, shuddering breath, her shoulders bowing. "Of course we don't have any choice," she whispers.

Despite that 'of course,' Father Ben looks mightily relieved, to me. "Put the rifles into the gun cabinet, then," he says. "They're, uh, less likely to go astray, that way."

Darryl throws him a sour look—clearly he's more worried about them getting used than lost. But she places her palm on the scanner and in a moment Josh, hers, and my rifles are all nestled inside.

"Wait, give me the pyx," says Father Ben, holding out his hand as she moves to close the door again.

Silently, she places her hand on the scanner again, genuflects, opens the explosives box, then gives Father Ben an 'over to you' wave towards it, kneeling.

Father Ben moves swiftly that way and genuflects as well, then pushes the feather-fabric curtain to one side. "Have you two eaten recently?"

Eaten? I'm not sure we even had *breakfast*.

"No," I say, since Darryl is shaking her head silently and Father Ben is intent on the pyx he's now holding.

"Then if you are in a fit state..."

Belatedly, I join Darryl on my knees as Father Ben carefully breaks the Host in three. He's changed the Host each time we've seen him, though he always says the long-life communion wafers used by rural priests are almost incorruptible. Darryl and I each receive a piece and he consumes the third, then he checks the pyx carefully for crumbs before placing it back in the tabernacle for safe keeping.

"HABITAT VEHICLE, YOU ARE SURROUNDED. PUT DOWN YOUR WEAPONS, OPEN THE DOORS AND PREPARE TO BE BOARDED OR WE WILL COMMENCE THE REMOVAL OF YOUR SHUTTERS."

"Harry, come here..." Darryl moves into the cab doorway, gathering me behind her protectively. She waits for Father Ben to close the tabernacle and the gun cabinet before reaching across to touch the side door control.

"Show your hands, both of you," says Father Ben, raising his, open and empty.

Uncertainly, I raise mine into view on either side of Darryl's protective head—I'm almost as tall as she is, now—and she holds hers out, as well.

"Put down any weapons!" yells a voice through the

doorway. A helmeted policeman's head comes into view and a pistol, raised high to cover the inside of the 'Vi. And a second guy. After peering suspiciously at us, they climb in, followed by two more, who immediately close the side-door behind them. Worried about us running away or about something coming in and eating them?

The first two grab Father Ben, pulling his hands roughly behind his back as they fasten handcuffs around his wrists.

"Hey!" I protest. "What are you *doing?*"

"It's okay, Harry," says Father Ben, his face now pressed against the wall as they search him. "It's fine. This is how they deal with adults, okay? Everything will be fine."

Fine? This is his definition of *fine*? I guess he's just trying to make me feel better.

As soon as they turn him around again, Father Ben's eyes dart to the officer with the most stripes on his shoulder, who's approaching Darryl—who's still blocking the cab doorway. Is she trying to protect Josh, too?

"Sergeant?" says Father Ben. "The kid in there, on the bed, he's really sick. Badly infected wound. Can't put his hands up or anything. He's unarmed, okay, and he needs to get to the hospital immediately. Are you hearing me?"

The officer nods curtly. "Sick, unarmed, got'ya,

padre. Not a kid, though, is he? The *kids* are out here."

"Heck, man, he's more innocent than any city-boy I ever met. Please don't hurt him."

With a snort, the policeman shoots a pointed look at Darryl, then peers behind us, his expression black.

"Move aside," he orders.

DARRYL

"Let him through, Darryl," says Father Ben, managing to remain composed despite his cuffed hands and the fact that a policeman grips each arm.

Reluctantly, I shift to the side, keeping Harry behind me, afraid they'll drag him away.

Before he can move past me, the officer's radio crackles. "Sir, the cab door's opening, we've got movement..."

I swing around, my eyes searching for Josh. Heck, he *has* got the door open! All that shouting on the Intercar must have woken him and he was lucid enough to understand what was going on... He slides from his sleeping bag, falling to the ground far below in a jumbled heap. *Outage*, that must've hurt! Somehow, he makes it to his feet, lurching a few hunched-over steps...

"*Sick and unarmed!*" Father Ben's yelling frantically. "Don't shoot him!"

My heart contracts. They wouldn't?

"Hold your fire," snaps the officer, into his radio. "Suspect is believed to be unarmed and not a threat."

My heart starts beating again. Josh's legs give way under him, dropping him in a heap once more. He makes one last, helpless, heart-crushing attempt to crawl, then slumps motionless. Unconscious?

"Will you *please* call an ambulance?" says Father Ben.

The officer moves to the door and shuts it, then touches his radio again. "Start setting up a temporary fence so we can retrieve the perp," he barks. He shoots a look at Harry and me. I mouth *please* because I don't know what else to do. He sighs and touches the radio again. "And get an ambulance here, ASAP."

So they put up their little portable fence. Why they bother when there's a HabVi right here with a turret they could use, don't ask me. They leave Josh lying out there until it's up, but they won't let any of us go to him, however many times we ask. We even offer to go and bring him in, but no, they want their little fence. Finally, it's operational and they open the side-door again.

An ambulance now stands beside one of the police cars, thank God! With some difficulty, they trundle a gurney over the rough ground to him, lower it, and move him onto it.

Unfortunately, he's come around by now. He

struggles, pitifully weak and ineffective. He sobs; he *begs* them to let him go. The fear in his voice...it overloads me with pain; I can barely breathe. I try to go to him but the policemen hold me back, keeping me in the 'Vi. I struggle, but they're too strong.

"Don't give up, Josh!" I yell, since my voice is the only thing that can reach him, but I'm not sure he hears, lost in terror and delirium. "Don't give up! *Please don't give up!*"

But faced with this, he'll only live now if the doctors *make* his body recover, won't he?

Apparently unaffected by his pleading, they just wheel him to the ambulance. Give him some injection or other to shut him up and load him inside.

"Don't give up, Josh!"

Away it goes. It's the most horrible thing I've ever had to watch. My insides shake and tremble. Harry's shaking and sobbing. I pull free of the cops and wrap my arms around him. I *refuse* to cry. Hunters don't break down during a crisis. I've got to stay strong, be calm, for Harry.

"At least he's on his way to the hospital now," I whisper to Harry. "At least there's a chance he'll be okay."

Okay? In prison? Josh?

Where there's life, there's hope. Isn't that a saying?

"Okay, get the priest moving." The officer jabs a

finger at Father Ben and the two officers move him towards the side door.

"Bye, kids," says Father Ben, doing an—almost—perfect impression of being unfazed. "I'll look you up as soon as I can, okay?"

I watch him go, watch them load him into a police car and drive away, unable to come up with a single word. Harry's still shaking, sniffing, valiantly trying to get his tears under control.

Oh, Josh...

The officer's taken out a long-range communicator and raised it to his ear. It's the third time he's done it, but no one's answered. Until now.

"Ah, Ms. Matthews. Yes, that's right. We have them."

Fernanda. I'm unprepared for the wave of pure rage that swamps me. This is the second time that woman will have taken our home from us and upended our lives. I want to rush across the 'Vi, I want to snatch that fancy city communicator, I want to scream into it, something horrible and hurtful, I want to smash it to pieces on the floor...

Shaking, I stay where I am, and carry on holding Harry tight. Father Ben's right. Anything like that will only make things worse. If she was actually *here*...I'm not sure I coulda controlled myself.

"Okay. Yes. We'll see you there," the officer is

saying.

I glance around as Kiko rustles slightly from the cab where he's now hiding. Hang on...they won't let me keep Kiko, will they? I move to the console, towing Harry with me, and reach for the messaging app.

"Hey, what are you doing?" demands the officer.

"We're not allowed pets, right?" My voice comes out thin and strained. "I need to send a message to my neighbor, so he can come in-city and collect my quadravian." I nod towards the cab.

The officer peers at Kiko, thinks for a moment, then nods. Letting out the breath I've been holding, I bend and type quickly.

Uncle Mau,

We've been caught. I'm not allowed a pet. If you possibly can, can you come as quick as you can, or Riley, or Sandra and meet us in-city (Exception) and take Kiko or they will send him to the pound? Thank you.

Darryl

I hit send without wasting time re-reading it, in case the cop changes his mind. Thankfully, we're in text-transfer range of a satellite and it goes immediately. Small mercies. What will they do with the 'Vi? It's Josh's property. They have to keep it for him, right?

The officer clears his throat. "The two of you, please pack your personal belongings ready to travel in-city.

Wait, take those big knives off your belts, first."

Silently, we obey. What else can we do? My hands shake as I place our hunting knives in the back of a cupboard, hoping they won't take them, everything shakes as I climb up into the cab bedroom and fish my carryall from a cupboard. The 'Vi has felt like home for a long time, but never so much as at this moment, when I know we're about to be taken away from it—even with the tabernacle empty. At least Our Lord won't be abandoned in there for who knows how long, so it's a good thing. I'll keep telling myself that.

Blindly, I shove my things into the bag. I add my blank leather hunter-style waistcoat, which I haven't had time to decorate yet, and as many handicrafting items as I can fit in. Kiko's things I put in another small bag, his cage collapsed and folded—hidden—at the bottom. When I climb down again, I go into the cab, put Kiko's leash on him and clip it to my shoulder. He'll be harder to take away from me if he's not conveniently contained in a cage. Uncle Mau will come in time. He will.

My foot touches Josh's rosary, lying on the floor. His dad's rosary—so precious to him. Should I put it into the glovebox? What if it goes missing? After a moment of indecision, I slip it into my pocket instead. I don't think they'll take items like that from me.

"Bring one of the little cages for Tiny," I tell Harry,

when I go back into the living area. "Uncle Mau can take charge of him, too."

He nods, mutely. He's stopped crying, but his face is grubby with tear-streaks.

"What's that for?" demands the officer, as Harry puts a very small cage with his bag. "Another pet?"

"No, not a pet," says Harry quickly. "A live asset."

"But what is it?"

"Just a chick." Harry takes Tiny out and displays him to the man, claws hidden in his cupped hand. "Harmless. Just needs to go to the zoo."

"*What* is it?"

Harry's eyes dart nervously, but he has to answer. "Uh, velociraptor. Only a few days old. Totally harmless."

"*Raptor*? We're not taking that in-city."

Harry shoots me a desperate look. I feel so numb, I can hardly think beyond Josh, and leaving the 'Vi, but I have to help.

"The man who's collecting my pet can take it straight to the zoo," I say, trying to sound very calm and reasonable.

"And this man, he has a live capture license that permits him to transport velociraptors through city limits?"

Like Josh has... I swallow. "Uh...no, but this cage, see, it's fully certified. The chick will be inside it the whole time. It's not far to the zoo. They'll be pleased to have it..."

"I don't care how pleased they will be, it's completely illegal. Just let it go."

"He's too young!" Harry cries. "Did you hear me; he's only a few days old!"

"That's *enough*!" The officer snatches Tiny from Harry's hands and lobs him out the door. The little chick plummets into a patch of bushes, a tiny peep trailing behind him.

"You may have hurt him!" yells Harry, dashing for the doorway and leaping out.

It's no use, of course. With Kiko on my shoulder I have to scramble down more slowly and by the time I'm on the ground Harry is being bundled into a police car. I rush around and leap in the other side, determined not to let them separate us. When I peer out past Harry, I can see a couple of cops carrying our bags over. They put them in the trunk. And then, just like that, we're driving away.

I twist around, staring at the huge, metallic grey HabVi as it falls behind us. Will it ever be our home again? Is Josh going to be okay? Without Josh, it's nothing but a cold, utilitarian vehicle.

Harry stares back at the bushes as though trying to spot that poor twice-abandoned chick, then stares at the 'Vi as well. Once we're out of sight he faces forward and looks fixedly ahead, his jaw clenched. Refusing to sob anymore. Silent tears track down his cheeks.

I don't think I could cry right now. How can I be so numb and in such pain all at once? I reach out and grip Harry's hand tightly. I don't know what's going to happen. They're probably going to separate us when we reach the city.

But right now, for just a little longer, we're still together.

I squeeze Harry's hand. "Let's say a chaplet for Josh," I murmur.

So we do.

Together.

+

Don't miss unSPARKed 8:

A DIFFERENT KIND OF CAMOUFLAGE

The Boy Who Knew

FRIENDS IN HIGH PLACES: CARLO ACUTIS

DEAD? DEFINE DEAD.

"You have leukemia."

Daniel's just received the worst news a teen can get. The adults in his life are crumbling under the shock. In desperation, he turns to his parish priest for help and is introduced to a boy his age, Carlo Acutis—who just happens to be dead.

Daniel's convinced the priest is wasting his time. But as he struggles to come to terms with his uncertain future an unlikely friendship develops between him and the holy dead boy—who may not be quite so dead after all.

The Boy Who Knew is the first title in Carnegie Medal nominee Corinna Turner's new 'Friends in High Places' series. If you've always been interested in the saints but find dry biographies boring and hard to get through, this fast-paced story is for you.

"Powerful and inspiring."
SUSAN PEEK, author of the God's Forgotten Friends series

"beautifully honest"
KARINA FABIAN, author of *Discovery*

READ ON FOR A SNEAK PEEK

"You have leukemia."

I keep seeing the doctor's eyes over his mask, darting from me to my parents. I keep hearing his words in my head. Mum burst into tears. Dad started pounding on the doctor's desk with his fists. Me, I just sat there.

Leukemia. How can I have leukemia? I'm fifteen. Stuff that bad doesn't happen to people my age, right?

But the tiredness... The bruising...

"You have leukemia."

When we got home from the hospital, Mum started getting ready for the Vigil Mass as usual. Dad never comes along, these days, but tonight...tonight he started yelling at Mum *how could she possibly think there was a God if He could let this happen to me? How could she think He was good?* And Mum shouted back that *God was my only hope, couldn't he see that? Did he want me to die?*

They were still screaming at each other when I slipped out of the house and walked to church. I don't think I've ever come to church on my own before. I felt really self-conscious. Any other week I'd have grabbed the chance to skip Mass. Today, I am angry with God, I suppose? But I'm also really, really scared. And I just wanted to escape the shouting.

Mum never showed up for Mass. I got a text during the first reading: *Daniel, where are you?* I texted back: *At church.* An old lady glared at me over the top of her un-environmentally friendly single-use mask.

Then I fell asleep during the homily. I'm just so tired all the time. I got glared at again.

Now everyone's gone, and I'm still sitting here. I'm afraid to go home in case they're still arguing. Or in case they want to talk about it all. I feel numb. I haven't even taken my mask off, though I'm alone.

"You have leukemia."

"Do you want Daniel to die*?"*

Am I going to die? Words from one of the readings I heard before I nodded off come into my mind: *There is no need to worry; but if there is anything you need, pray for it.*

"God, please don't let me die," I whisper.

God doesn't reply. Maybe Dad's right. Pulling my mask of at last, I shove it into my pocket, hands shaking.

"God, I'm scared."

Nothing. Well, except that the numbness shatters and, suddenly, I really *feel* the fear, turning my belly into a black hole, cold as a...a...a morgue?

I bury my face in my hands as the sobs rip from me. *Am I going to die, Lord?*

Distant footsteps from the front of the church.

They pause, then tread briskly along the aisle. Towards me. Oh no.

I wipe my face, desperately trying to stop the gasping, heaving sobs. Snot smears my sleeve. Yuck.

"Hi, Daniel."

Reluctantly, I glance up, my shoulders still shuddering. It's Father Thomas. He's young and kinda cool, sweeping around in his long black dress—sorry, *cassock*—without a trace of embarrassment. I wish I had his total lack of self-consciousness.

"Hi, Father." My voice wobbles. *Play it cool, Daniel. Just pretend you're fine and get up and leave.*

"Are you okay?"

"No." I'm shaking my head. What happened to leaving? And then I'm blurting, "I've got leukemia."

His lips part as though I just punched him in the gut. "Oh, Daniel..." He settles into the next wide-spaced pew, sitting sideways to face me, eyes narrowed in concern. "Heck, I thought you were going to say bullying or something. That's a hard thing to face, at your age. When are you starting treatment? Did they say...what the prognosis is?"

"Prognosis?" I sound like an idiot. Oh, whether I'm going to live or die, he means. "Oh, uh...well, I just got the preliminary test result today. After more tests on Monday morning, the specialists make a plan and I see them the next Monday and...well, that's when they'll tell me...y'know. They think I'll start treatment almost at once."

"That's good. Just time for a novena, too."

"What?"

He pulls out his wallet and flicks through several

business cards before pulling one out. "This is the saint for you. Well, a Blessed, technically. In fact, he's not a Blessed until next Saturday, so I shouldn't really be giving these new cards out yet, but under the circumstances. Here. Almost-Blessed Carlo Acutis. He had leukemia when he was fifteen. Best prayer buddy you could have right now. I think there's a novena on his website."

He sees my vague look. "A novena's when you team up with a saint for nine days to pray for something."

"Oh yeah, I remember." I accept the card and slip it into my pocket, though I'm not sure I want it. Now the numbness has gone, I am starting to feel pretty mad at God. Isn't He supposed to love me? A wire of white-hot rage tightens painfully around my insides, and I scowl towards the tabernacle. Dad's right, how could He let this happen to me? What did I ever do to Him?

"Have you ever made a pot?" asks Father Thomas, suddenly. "Or a painting?"

What? "Uh, I make 3D art on my computer. Loads of it."

"Ah, that's right. I knew you were an artist of some kind. Say if you created a 3D pot, then. Did anyone force you to make it?"

I look at him blankly. "No. I just do it because I want to."

"Could you, like, virtually smash it?"

"In my program? Sure. More or less." A surge of happiness flows through me at the thought of my state-of-the-art 3D design program and extensive inventory of quality assets...then wilts. What good will it all do me if I can't beat this thing?

"Could you take the pieces of your ex-pot and make them into a mosaic that was far, far more beautiful?"

"If I wanted to."

"And that would be okay? Breaking your pot and remaking it into something better?"

"Of course. It's my pot. I made it, right?"

"And then you could keep your beautiful mosaic forever, right?"

Forever? I may not have a *year*, for all I know... Belatedly, I figure out what he's on about. "Oh, very clever! I'm not a *pot!* It's not the same!"

"No, it's not the same," Father Thomas agrees, unperturbed. "We're far, far more important to God than some 3D pot. Or even a real one. He loves every single hair on our heads—and he knows exactly how many there are."

"Great!" I snap, leaping up from the pew and storming away from his infuriating calm. I yell over my shoulder, "I'll be sure to remember that when they start falling out!"

But I catch his soft words, just before I slip through the door.

"I hope you do."

**Get THE BOY WHO KNEW from
your favorite retailer today!**

ABOUT THE AUTHOR

Corinna Turner has been writing since she was fourteen and likes strong protagonists with plenty of integrity. Although she spends as much time as possible writing, she cannot keep up with the flow of ideas, for which she offers thanks—and occasional grumbles!—to the Holy Spirit. She is the author of over twenty-five books, including the Carnegie Medal Nominated I Am Margaret series, and her work has been translated into four languages. She was awarded the St. Katherine Drexel award in 2022.

She is a Lay Dominican with an MA in English from Oxford University and lives in the UK. She is a member of a number of organizations, including the Society of Authors, Catholic Teen Books, Catholic Reads, the Angelic Warfare Confraternity, and the Sodality of the Blessed Sacrament. She used to have a Giant African Land Snail, Peter, with a 6½" long shell, but now makes do with a cactus and a campervan.

Get in touch with Corinna...

Facebook: Corinna Turner

Twitter: @CorinnaTAuthor

Don't forget to sign up for

NEWS

&

FREE SHORT STORIES
at:

www.UnSeenBooks.com

All Free/Exclusive content subject to availability.

www.ingramcontent.com/pod-product-compliance
Lightning Source LLC
Chambersburg PA
CBHW030806190726
48285CB00003B/1054